The Bus of Dreams

The Bus

of Dreams

Stories by
Mary Morris

Houghton Mifflin Company   Boston
1985

All the characters in these stories, including the narrator,
are fictitious; any resemblance between them and real persons,
living or dead, is purely coincidental.

Library of Congress Cataloging in Publication Data
Morris, Mary, date
    The bus of dreams.

    I. Title.
PS3563.O87445B8   1985   813'.54   84-27883
ISBN 0-395-36236-9

Printed in the United States of America

Q 10 9 8 7 6 5 4 3 2 1

The author is grateful for permission to quote from "Agua Sexual" by Pablo
Neruda, translated by Robert Bly and James Wright, from *Neruda and Vallejo:
Selected Poems*, edited by Robert Bly (Beacon Press, 1971).

The following stories were previously published, as follows:
    "The Banana Fever," *Transatlantic Review*, 1977.
    "Links," *TriQuarterly*, 1981.
    "Copies," *The Agni Review*, 1983, reprinted in *The Pushcart Prize, IX:
Best of the Small Presses*, 1984.
    "Conquering Space," *Black Warrior Review*, 1984.
    "Orphans of the Storm," *The Paris Review*, 1984.
    "Shining Path," *The Agni Review*, 1985.
    "The Watermelon People," *Confrontation*, 1985.

for Richard

Acknowledgments

I would like to thank Sharon Dunn and John Clayton for their editorial suggestions and *The Agni Review* for its continuing support. I would also like to thank MeKeel McBride, Richard Falk, and Shigeo Tobita for their comments and criticism. I would like to thank Jane Supino for her wisdom, my agents Lynn Nesbit and Amanda Urban for their help, and Frances Apt, my manuscript editor, and Helena Bentz, chief of manuscript editing at Houghton Mifflin, for their great attention to detail and their care in the preparation of the manuscript. I would like to give special thanks to Nan Talese, my editor, for her insight, her compassion, and her patience. I would also like to express my gratitude to my friends in Central and South America, especially Epigmenio Mercado Nava, Gilmar Gonzalez Salinas, Carol Wise, Guadalupe Martinez and her children, and the many others — too numerous to name — who showed me the way.

Contents

I look at secretive dreams,
I let the straggling days come in,
and the beginning also, and memories also,
like an eyelid held open hideously
I am watching.

— Pablo Neruda

Conquering Space

FOR A TIME when I was growing up, my father was in charge of fuel transport at Cape Canaveral, before it was renamed Cape Kennedy. After the Korean War, he'd studied engineering and the Army had paid for his training. My father felt it was his duty to pay the Army back, so for a while we lived in Florida near the space center and my father thought about fuel.

We lived in a small, flat, pink house on the edge of a small swamp and in that house my parents fought a great deal. The main thing they fought about was that my mother hated living in Florida. She could find nothing charming about the dog races or the coconut palm that grew in our front lawn. She hated the humidity and the merciless sun. We had been moving from city to city since before my brother, Trevor, and my sister, Eleanore, were born, and we had finally settled down, my mother thought, in St. Louis, when my father took the job with NASA.

We drove to Florida in our station wagon with a trailer hooked to it along a road that stretched from the Canadian border to Key West, and the day we arrived my mother threatened to pack us all up and move back north. She waved at my father and threw him a kiss as he unpacked the van. "Go ahead. You stay here. I'll wait for you, I promise." But he'd just taken our kitchen chairs out of the van and headed toward the pink house we were to live in, acknowledging her plea only with a minisalute.

Unlike my mother, my father loved Florida. He loved the ocean breezes, the constant season, and our front lawn. He loved to cut the lawn, trim the hedges. He said it relaxed him. He said that the lawn and house should be neat and pass inspection, just like a soldier's bunk and beard. My father liked to trim the lawn every day when he came home from work. He had a crew cut then, because he worked for the Army, and my mother used to tease him because his head looked like the lawn.

My father's job was highly technical, and we were warned, whenever we were bad, that it was also highly dangerous. Though I've never understood the fine points very well and always lost interest when they were being explained to me, my father was the one who saw to it that just the right amounts of liquid hydrogen and liquid oxygen were fed into the spacecraft. At any moment, we were told, our father could be blown to bits, and how would we feel if we hadn't been nice to him in the morning before he left the house.

Actually his work was somewhat dangerous. He was the engineer in charge of transferring fuel from tanks to spacecraft. He told us, when he took the job, that he was to the space launch what the anesthesiologist was to an operation, but my mother, who'd had her share of disappointments, was less impressed; he was, my mother once said, a sophisticated gas station attendant.

The year we moved to Florida was the year I was old enough to get my driver's permit and to begin learning how to drive. My father told me that driving a car was a very difficult, important task and that he was going to teach me. The family car was an old Ford station wagon with fake wood paneling and it smelled of babies and our dog, Oscar. Oscar was big with bad breath and an odor about him that could not be gotten rid of, which we later recognized as the smell of incurable disease. Oscar was old and dying and the car stank of him as my father taught me how to drive.

My father always came home from work early in the midafternoon and did a half-hour of calisthenics. "All right, Janet," he'd say to me, "count the first sixty." And he'd do sixty quick sit-ups, then make me pound on his belly to show me that it was taut as a drum. Then he'd mow the lawn, and when he was done with that, he'd say, "Now, young lady, ready for your lesson?"

The first thing we did was drive to the Sinclair station and get the car filled up with gas. I would drive and my father would sit beside me, the driver's manual open on his lap, waiting for me to make a mistake so that he could read me the rule I'd just broken. "You did not properly signal your right-hand turn before you entered traffic." He was a difficult man to please and I always wanted to do well. I approached my lessons with the solemnity of a novice embarking upon her vows. I'd drive slowly into the station, where a green-eyed boy in overalls with grease all over his face filled up our tank.

It was crucial to my father that the tank be filled at all times. He wouldn't even drive to the beach, which was half a mile away from our house, without a full tank. It was a kind of theme in our childhood. We knew that any quiet nap in the car, any terrific joke or great story someone was telling, could be interrupted by a sudden need to stop for gas. And if we complained, my father would say, "You'll see. Some night you'll be out on a dark highway or driving down Alligator Alley, and someone will have forgotten to fill it up for you the night before. Then you'll appreciate this." But it wasn't just the car that had to be filled. It was the little motor on the lawn mower. It was the bathtub and coffee cups. My father had a real horror of empty spaces.

After the car was filled up, my father would say to me, "All right, now, we're going to work on a right-hand turn into a left-hand lane." Or we were going to work on parallel parking or passing a moving vehicle on a two-lane highway. Whatever it was we were working on, we wouldn't go home until I'd mastered it. When we went out for the parallel parking lesson, I didn't get it right until ten o'clock that night. "What are you doing?" my mother screamed when he brought me home, exhausted and starving. "Getting her ready for the Marines?"

My father smiled, opening a bottle of Scotch and pouring three fingers. "My little Janet is tough," he said. "She can take it."

The night my father told us a man was going to walk on the moon was the same night I heard my parents fighting in a way that frightened me for the first time. It was one of those sticky, hot Florida evenings, though every evening in Florida was the same, it seemed; only some were hotter than others, and my father always insisted we eat dinner, unless there was a downpour, on the patio. So we sat, night after night, in the dark, swatting the mosquitoes under the stars, which my father gazed at as if he were somehow closer to them than the rest of us were. He listened to us chatter on about our schools and our lessons. He listened to my mother talk about what had happened at the grocery that day while he drank his Scotch and watched the stars.

He liked to ask us in the midst of whatever we were talking about what important work we had done that day.

If we told him we had solved a math problem that had been plaguing us or gotten a part in some school play, he seemed pleased, but he always managed to turn whatever we told him into an occasion for a lecture on good work. "Work is what counts in this world," he began his discourse that evening. "I grew up during the Depression." The Depression, we knew, had ruined his father. "I know what it is not to have work. Let me tell you, you've got to have a skill. Just do one thing better than anybody else. That's what counts."

He sat up very straight and puffed up his chest so that he seemed to grow before our eyes. We all turned toward him, which was what he wanted. Then he leaned forward and whispered, "Something incredible is going to happen . . ."

Trevor flung his arms onto the table and bounced in his chair. "What? What?" He was twelve and the middle child; everything he did then seemed excessive. Eleanore, who was the youngest and copied whatever Trevor did, also began bouncing, shrieking, "What? What's gonna happen?"

My father hesitated, looked very serious, took a deep drink. Then he looked up at the sky. "A man is going to walk on the moon." He tapped his index finger against his sternum. Kennedy had recently taken office and one of his promises was that man would reach the moon before the end of the decade, but it never occurred to us that our father would have anything to do with it.

Our mother was swatting mosquitoes and passing plates around. "Janet," she said, "finish your chicken. Trevor, eat your salad. Eleanore, quit mushing up your potato like that." I could tell she was annoyed, because she referred to us individually like a drill sergeant.

"How?" Trevor almost shrieked. "How's he going to walk on the moon?"

My father looked placidly at the sky. "He's going to go

up in a spaceship and it's going to land on the moon. And
I'm going to see he gets there."

"What about Schlecter?" my mother said. "I'm sure he'll
have something to say about this." We knew there was a
Colonel Schlecter, a man we'd never met but had been
raised to hate, who stood in the way of our father and
success. If our father got a man to the moon, it would be
only because Schlecter gave him the go-ahead.

Ignoring her comment, he pointed in the direction of the
moon. We all looked. It was a lovely, golden moon that
was almost full but not quite. We were enjoying looking
at it, imagining our father sending someone all the way
there, when our mother suddenly stood up and took the
drink out of his hand. "For Christ's sake, Jim," she said,
"I can't stand having you fill their heads with this nonsense."

"What do you know about it," he snapped.

My mother looked at him and sighed. "No man is going
to walk on the moon and you're certainly not going to be
the one who sends him there."

She sat back down again and patted her hair, which had
turned frizzy in the Florida sun. My father threw his napkin onto his plate, got up, and let the porch door slam behind him as he walked into the house. We finished dinner
in silence, none of us daring to look up or to watch our
mother, fidgeting nervously with her fork.

Our father, she had told us many times, was a dreamer
and we had to take what he said with a grain of salt. In
all fairness to my mother, she had been engaged to an insurance broker when she met my father and her parents
had approved of the marriage to the insurance broker. But
then my father returned from the Army and arrived in
Milwaukee one night. He was friends with her brother, and
he swept my mother off her feet. He promised her he was
going to be rich and do great things. He told her he had a

great career ahead of him as an engineer. He promised her she'd see the world and he'd be a faithful lover. He'd only been able to come through on the last.

When we went back into the house after dinner, mosquito-bitten and sweaty, I saw my father in the middle of the living room, lifting weights. He did this often, but this time he seemed to be doing it with some special force. His face was red and puffy and he kept breathing in and out, gasping for breath. His muscles were strained beneath his T-shirt; I thought it would rip in half.

The day my father taught me how to pass a moving vehicle on a two-lane highway, I almost killed us both. He'd come home from work a little later than usual and seemed agitated. He said something important was going to be happening down at the space center soon. He seemed so upset that I suggested we forget about my driving lesson that day, but he said, "You've gotta stick to it. If you don't stick to it, you'll never learn."

We let Oscar jump into the back seat and drove off to the Sinclair station, with its dinosaur sign out front. The green-eyed boy in the blue overalls with grease on his forehead waited on us. "Fill it up, Mr. Hamilton?" the boy said.

"Fill it up," my father said, without raising his eyes from the driver's training manual.

The boy took the hose and put it in the gas tank and I felt the car begin to take in the gas. The smell of gasoline was in the air. My father sat beside me, flipping nervously through the manual, his nails bitten down to the quick. As he turned the pages, I saw red scaly spots on his hands from rubbing. I wondered what made him do that and decided it was the pressures of being a fuel transport engineer.

The green-eyed boy dipped his squeegee in water and began wiping the windshield. The windshield was dusty, and the squeegee made a squeaky sound. As he wiped, the window became clearer and I saw his gentle eyes. His body stretched smoothly across the hood of our car and I smiled at him. "How're the lessons coming?" he asked. My father handed him his credit card and the boy smiled back at me. The pump clicked as it came to a halt. I wondered if the boy could go up in smoke at any moment, the way we'd been told our father could.

We drove out onto a narrow strip of highway that cut across Florida like Alligator Alley, and my father told me I was going to learn how to pass cars that day. He explained, the way he always did, in meticulous detail, how I was to keep my eye on the road ahead, accelerate, pass the car, wait until it appeared in my rearview mirror, put on my turn signal before returning to my lane, and so on.

My mind wasn't on turn signals and acceleration as I sped along the road. Rather, it was on the green-eyed boy who'd leaned across the windshield and smiled at me. And it was his face I saw ahead of me, not the oncoming car, as I tried to pass on a two-lane highway.

"Step on it, Janet!" my father shouted. Oscar hung between us, panting, and my father with one swift movement, a movement as graceful as any I'd ever seen, hurled the dog into the far reaches of the station wagon, grabbed the wheel, and floored it. Somehow he managed to get us back into our lane, amidst the screeching of brakes and the beeping of horns, as a Mustang, traveling at breakneck speed, swerved to avoid crashing into us, head-on.

My father drove a few more feet, then got the car off the road, pulled over, and shook me. It was the only time in my life anyone had ever laid a hand on me, and I think it stunned both of us. He put his hands on my shoulders and shook me until my head wobbled back and forth and I thought my arms would come loose. "What were you thinking about?" he shouted. "Not the road, that's for sure.

Not about driving. Don't you ever again drive without having your mind on it, do you understand me? Do you understand?" All the time he spoke he was shaking me; I was amazed at the strength in his arms.

He made me get in the back seat, and, as Oscar blew his sour breath into my crying face, my father broke the speed limit and drove us home. When we walked in, my mother took one look at me, then at him. "She goddamn almost got us killed."

He began drinking earlier that day, and later in the evening, as we all were watching television, my father leaned down near me, and his breath stank the way Oscar's did. "I'm sorry," he said. "I lost my temper."

That night as I drifted to sleep I heard my parents fighting in their room. It was one of those awful, hot nights, and Eleanore and I were sleeping with our door open, but I couldn't make out what they said. Then the door to my parents' room slammed and heavy footsteps pounded down the stairs. I waited all night for the footsteps to tiptoe back up the stairs again, but they never did.

The day I got my driver's license, the boy from the pumping station asked me out. I'd gone to get the car filled up for a solo ride, and as he leaned across the windshield, removing some bird droppings, he said, "Wanta go out tonight?" His name was Tim and he was a high school student from Daytona. He drove a souped-up car with a lot of horsepower. He picked me up in a seersucker suit, with all the grease carefully removed from his hands and with his hair slicked back. My father didn't recognize him as they shook hands and Tim escorted me out the door. "You drive carefully now," my father said.

We ate a pizza and saw a bad Western. Then Tim asked if I wanted to go for a ride. He pulled me close as we drove along a strip of unlit highway that cut Florida in half. The wind whipped through the palms, and the moon had never seemed so bright as it did that night. I threw my head back against the seat of the convertible and watched the sky until we ran out of gas.

The car just sputtered and died somewhere on the strip, and there was nothing in sight. Tim and I sat, with our arms around each other, waiting for a car to pass. The highway was dark and the night balmy. We listened to the radio and he kissed me until an old couple in a jalopy came along. We flagged them down and they drove us, creeping along at twenty miles an hour, to the nearest gas station.

It was midnight when I walked in the door. My father sat, staring at the television, a glass of Scotch in his hand. "I don't want any explanations," he said. "You will simply never be late again in your entire life. Is that clear?"

"It's clear, but . . ." I wanted to explain about driving down the road and the wind in the palms, but he raised his index finger up to his face.

"No buts. Get to bed."

Tim later told me that my father drove to the gas station the next day and stared at him for a long time. As he handed Tim his credit card he said, "You're the one who took my daughter out last night." And he drove away.

When he got home, he walked in and screamed at me, "What were you doing out all night with a gas station attendant?"

My mother stepped in. "He's a nice boy," she said. "There's nothing wrong with her going out with him." It was four in the afternoon, but she wore a bathrobe and had her hair in little pincurls all over her yellow head. Her hair had turned to some kind of straw in the Florida humidity, and all she did was sit home and put rinses on it.

"You will not see that boy again." He pointed at me.

My mother wrapped her bathrobe more tightly around her. "Let her make her mistakes now!" she shouted back.

"Let her find out what she wants before it's too late."

He glared at her, then turned to me and spoke very carefully. "And you're grounded for a week for being late."

"Yes, sir," I said and fled to my room.

Later, my mother came and sat down at the edge of my bed. She patted my foot. "You know, don't you?"

I didn't know, but I nodded anyway.

"We haven't been getting along for a while."

"I've noticed," I said.

"I think his career is falling apart."

I nodded again. I didn't really understand all of this, but it seemed to me that something was falling apart. "Don't leave him," I said. "He means well."

My mother sighed, patted my foot once more, and got up. She still had the pincurls in her head. "You're the only one who's old enough to understand." And she left.

A few nights later I lay in bed and heard my parents arguing again. Their voices rose from the kitchen, and I went downstairs, planning to use the pretext of wanting a glass of milk before bed. I tiptoed down and heard my father saying, "I'm not taking any orders from Schlecter. I'm not taking any orders from anyone."

"No." My mother spoke back to him in the kind of whisper that is really a shout. "And it's costing you your job and everything else." I peeked around the corner and saw my parents in what at first I took to be an embrace. My father had his hands pressed firmly on her arms, and my mother's head was thrown back as if she were about to be kissed on the lips. And then I saw my father shake her as he'd shaken me the day on the road when I'd almost killed us both.

He shook her and said, "You just don't understand."

My mother struggled in his grip and finally broke away. "You're drunk," she said. I tiptoed back up the stairs.

It must have been four in the morning when my father woke us. Trevor was already dressed. He rubbed his eyes and complained. He hated to be awakened, and Eleanore was almost impossible to wake. But I had only teetered on the brink of sleep that night, and waking me was easy. I was almost ready to go. My father shook me gently. "Come on. We're going somewhere. But be quiet."

The four of us shuffled downstairs, and I saw from the condition of the living room — the blankets and pillows tossed about, glasses everywhere, ashtrays filled with smoldering butts — that he'd probably been up all night. He moved through the living room with exaggerated precision and his warm breath blew against us as he helped us into the car. I sat beside him in the front seat. We were cold and he tossed dirty blankets from the garage across us. Oscar was barking, so my father let him jump in the back. "Oh, for Pete's sake," Eleanore said, sounding very much like my mother, "where're we going?" Trevor pushed Oscar away, saying, "He stinks. I wanta go back to sleep."

My father started the car and tore down the driveway in reverse, running over the white Day-Glo painted stone at the edge. The car thumped. Then he shifted abruptly into first gear and screeched down the street. "Maybe I should drive, Dad," I offered in a mature, adult way, but he shook his head. "I'm fine. I can drive. You be co-pilot."

We drove for what seemed like a long time and no one spoke. I began to grow bored. The highway was monotonous at night, and since I was co-pilot, I started to read the meters on the instrument panel. Our speed, our mileage, the gas gauge. That was when I grew afraid. The tank was only half full. I'd never known him to go anywhere with half a tank, and I knew he'd been driving much of the night. He was probably in no shape to be driving us anywhere now.

But still he drove and I sat beside him, with a mission

now. I was concentrating on the road, ready to grab the wheel at any moment. At last we reached a chain-link fence with a gate and a guard. The guard stepped forward and my father showed him a piece of identification. The guard nodded, opened the gate, and we drove onto a beach road. We drove for perhaps a mile before he stopped and told us to get out. We were on a strip of beach somewhere but we couldn't tell where. I knew it was government property, because he had shown his badge, but that was all I knew.

We sat on a dirty blanket in the sand and waited. My father said nothing. He just breathed heavily and kept looking at his watch. Then as day broke we saw something across the bay. It was tall and white and suddenly it was lit with floodlights. Eleanore and Trevor stood up and I leaned forward. My father smiled and checked his watch again. "Any second now," he said. We waited a few more minutes. Then suddenly there was a roar, and fire burst out of the rockets. We pressed our hands over our ears as the engines charged. Then, gracefully, as if it had simply decided it wanted to go elsewhere, the spacecraft rose.

The ship sailed straight up, white and flaming against the dark morning sky. It veered off above us, heading upward and away. My father, looking incredibly sad, watched it go. "Beautiful," he said, "that's really beautiful," over and over until the ship was out of sight and the din of its engines gone. Then he handed me the keys, and with the great care he had taught me, I drove us home.

When we walked into the living room, our mother was sitting in an armchair, her robe wrapped around her. She seemed haggard and washed out. She looked us over, and when she saw we were all right, she told us to go to bed.

But it was already morning, and I was sure I wouldn't be able to get back to sleep. I put on a jacket and decided to go for a walk. I tiptoed past the living room, where my father was sitting up, drink in hand, reading a book on the history of flight, but he heard me and motioned for me to come in. He put down his book and his drink. Then he clasped me by the arm. "Janet," he whispered, "in your lifetime, soon, a man is going to walk on the moon."

"Sure, Dad." I smiled and he smiled back, pleased that he had finally convinced one of us.

Then he looked up and a tear slid down his face. "It was beautiful, wasn't it? The launch."

"It was beautiful, Dad."

He nodded and seemed content. I thought of wiping the tear away, but I didn't. Instead, I let it keep sliding down his face. He still held his fingers tightly around my arm, and suddenly I wanted to get away from him. I shook myself free. I said, "I've gotta go."

He gave me a small salute as I went out the back door, which I let close gently on its hinges. I started to cut across the lawn to the street, but something made me turn back. I went around to the front of the house. When I got to the living room window, I peered in.

I put my eyes to the glass and saw my father, looking right at me. I waved and made faces. I jumped up and down and pressed my nose against the glass, but he didn't see me. He just lay on the sofa, staring straight ahead into space.

The Bus of Dreams

R AQUEL had been in Panama City for five weeks when
she saw the bus with her sister's picture painted on
the back. At first she thought it was a mistake, but then
she knew it couldn't be. So she ran after the bus. She ran
until she coughed in its exhaust, but it was no mistake.
Teresa had disappeared three years earlier, and Raquel had
come to find her, but she didn't expect it to be on the back
of a bus.

Every day as she went to and from her job in the Zona,
where she worked for the colonel and his wife, Raquel rode
the buses. She tried to ride a different bus each day, ever
since she saw Teresa's picture. She asked people when she
got on if they knew the bus she was looking for. Raquel
showed the drivers Teresa's snapshot, taken when she was
Queen of the Carnival. Some smiled and said she was
beautiful. Some said they wanted her picture on the back
of their bus.

But then one driver who had kind dark eyes looked at
the picture and nodded. He'd never seen the bus with Teresa's picture painted on the back, but he told her she had
to find the bus dream man. He would know. In Panama

every driver owns his own bus and every bus is different. When a man buys his bus, he takes it to a bus dream man. The bus dream man is a painter and a witch. On the back of the bus, he will paint the owner's secret desire. He paints objects of love, places that will be visited. He paints hopes, but never fears. And in the windows, he will put the names of the women loved. They say that the dream man in naming the dream brings the owner closer to finding his dream. They say that when the bus driver dies, he drives his bus right into heaven, where whatever the bus dream man painted comes true.

Raquel had never crossed the Isthmus of Panama before she came to the city, and she'd never been to the city before she began looking for Teresa. Teresa had been Queen of the Carnival just before she ran away. When Teresa was Queen, she'd worn a huge plumed headdress and a long feathery robe with green wings. She was a parrot. A sequined, feathered parrot. Because Teresa was so beautiful, their father had borrowed money from friends and from his sister in Colón. He took everything he had, which was very little, and put it into the dresses for Teresa's coronation.

   Their father had taken all his savings and all the money he borrowed and bought cloth and shoes from the Americans, and their mother had sewn every sequin and feather on the gown herself by hand. They had painted her deep green eyes with stripes of red and blue like a parrot's eyes, as if she were the great bird of the jungle. Raquel had been her lady-in-waiting. She'd dressed as a smaller green bird, and she sat beside Teresa on the float that carried them through the streets of their town.

   One day after the Carnival was over, Teresa said she was bored and that a friend of hers had a car. So Raquel and Teresa and the friend drove to San Lorenzo, the fort that perches above the Atlantic where Henry Morgan the pirate had invaded Panama. They drove through the U.S. Army base and the jungle and they drove along the edge of the fort that sits high above the sea. They watched the parrots fly wild through the ruins. Teresa had looked into one of the dungeons. She gazed deep into it, and Raquel saw her sister tremble and turn pale.

On the way back from the fort, two soldiers, wearing camouflage gear and carrying rifles, jumped out of the bushes and waved the girls down. They spoke broken Spanish and asked for a ride. They said they were on maneuvers and had to walk all the way back to the base. They showed them their guns and told jokes that made Teresa toss her head back and laugh. The soldiers told her she was very beautiful. She should be a star. For weeks Teresa sat, doing nothing in the house. Then one day she disappeared, leaving a note. It said she was going into pictures and she'd return when she was famous.

The first time Raquel saw her sister's picture on the back of a bus, she wondered if it was there because Teresa was already famous. She thought it should be easy to find a famous person. She showed her snapshot to everyone she met. She showed it to the bus drivers and policemen. She showed it to the colonel and his wife. Raquel had been fortunate to find work in the Zona. She had gone to hotels, looking for work as a maid, and one of the hotels had given her the name of the colonel and his wife. They hired her because she was a good cook and because she was quiet. Mrs. Randolph told Raquel when she hired her that it was important to be quiet. Raquel had been lucky to find this job, and she knew she'd be just as lucky to find Teresa.

Raquel liked her job in the Zona. She liked leaving the slums of Panama, where she lived in a small rented room. She liked the ride into the Canal Zone. The Zona was lush and green, and the American servicemen who lived in it lived in beautiful houses. They lived on the top of the hill and they had a view of the Canal and the jungles.

The house of the colonel and his wife was dark and cool and the garden was filled with trees. Pomegranates hung from the low branches and so did lemons and oranges. Raquel picked oranges from the trees and ate them for lunch. In the middle of the garden was a pond with goldfish, covered with dry leaves that fell from the trees, and the first thing Raquel did when she went to work for the Randolphs was to clear the leaves off the goldfish pond so that Mrs. Randolph could sit in her clean white blouse and poke her finger at the noses of the goldfish. Mrs. Randolph sat and stared, her finger stirring the water in endless circles that hypnotized the fish so that they seemed to have no choice but to follow the circles of Mrs. Randolph's finger.

Sometimes Mrs. Randolph talked to Raquel. Sometimes she didn't. But Raquel never talked to her unless Mrs. Randolph wanted to talk. Sometimes Mrs. Randolph just sat in the bedroom with the shades drawn, sipping long cool drinks. But sometimes Mrs. Randolph would ask Raquel to tell her about where she came from. And Raquel told the colonel's wife how she came from a village in the Interior where the buzzards clung to the trees and the men carried their machetes to bed with them. She told Mrs. Randolph how the heat was so strong it never left their house, even on a cool spring night. How the mosquitoes coated the rooms of their house like wallpaper, and how the people drank and bathed in the same river that was their sewer.

When Raquel told Mrs. Randolph these things, the colonel's wife would close her eyes and drift back into her darkened room for the rest of the day. But once Mrs. Randolph asked Raquel what she'd like to have if she could have anything. There were many things she wanted. She wanted to marry the young man she'd left behind in her town, the one whose mustache didn't grow and who wanted to be a teacher. And sometimes she thought she wanted to nurse the sick and other times she wanted to have five children. But Raquel considered Mrs. Randolph's question carefully, and finally she said, "I'd like to live in a house where the breeze blows through."

Mrs. Randolph closed her eyes and said, "There are other things in this world besides living in a house like this."

One day Raquel told Mrs. Randolph why she'd come to the city. She told Mrs. Randolph how her father had married the woman he loved when he was sixteen years old. Her mother had borne him twelve children, and eight had died of disease. Teresa was the oldest and her father's favorite. She told Mrs. Randolph how her sister had run away. Shortly after Teresa ran away, her mother died. Every morning her father went to the fruit plantation where he worked, and after Teresa left and her mother died, he walked with the hesitant walk of one trying to find something he thinks he has lost.

In the evenings he came home and sat on the front porch, drinking rum and carving small animals out of wood. He'd sit, surrounded by his battalion of small animals. He carved dogs and cats and small sheep and cows. He also carved animals he'd never seen, except in pictures. He made an animal with a long neck and another with a long nose. He made a huge, fat animal with a horn in the middle of its head. He did not believe these animals actually existed, but he told Raquel that if he were ever rich enough, he'd travel to the place where these animals lived.

One night as he sat on the porch, surrounded by his animals carved of wood, Raquel asked if there was anything she could do for him. He gazed down the empty, dusty streets of their town. Then he looked up at her with his sad gray eyes; Raquel feared the look would enter her and she would walk with his hesitant walk.

Raquel had taken a room near the old French quarter that was not unlike her room in the Interior. She had imagined

when she came to the city that she'd have a room that
overlooked a courtyard where the bougainvillea worked its
way to her window and, when she opened her window at
night, the breeze from the sea would blow in the scarlet
petals of bougainvillea and the night air of her room would
be filled with the scent of fresh flowers.

But she had looked for a week and in the end settled for
a room with a view of the next building, where the smell
of burning kerosense and frying fish entered, mingled with
the groans of old people and the muffled sounds of cou-
ples making love in the tropical heat. She'd taken a room
where she had to wipe the cobwebs off her face in the
morning and fight the bugs that crawled across her arms
as she slept in damp sheets on a damp mattress with the
smell of old mold and the impression of sad bodies.

She'd stared at herself in the cracked glass when she
moved in and knew that she was pretty, but not like Teresa. Teresa had silky black hair and ivory skin. Teresa
didn't have a mole on her right cheek, and her face was
sculpted, not flat and round like Raquel's. Raquel moved
into the room and unpacked her things. She unpacked the
tortoiseshell combs the boy she loved back home had given
her. She unpacked her shell beads and the white dress her
mother had embroidered. She unpacked the fotonovelas she
liked to read at night and pictures of Clark Gable and John
Travolta. She put these beside the pictures of her family
and of Teresa. She unpacked the rosary her grandmother
had given her and the small statue of the Virgin in a blue
robe, her trouble dolls and the amulets from the fortune-
teller in her town. She wiped away the cobwebs that would
return each morning and she settled in.

Raquel had also brought with her a small porcelain doll
with no arms. When Raquel and Teresa were little, they'd
kept a secret place. It was under the porch of an abandoned house, and they kept all kinds of things in their se-

cret place. They kept small stones and the feathers of birds, pits of fruit and bones of animals they'd eaten. They kept old forks and pieces of tin. And they kept the porcelain doll, which they dressed in scraps of cloth their mother gave them. They built the doll a house out of cardboard with large windows and a patio. But when Teresa got older, she lost interest in the secret place. So one day Raquel collected all their things and moved them in a sack into their house.

That was when Teresa introduced Raquel to the world of boys. Teresa was five years older, and sometimes when their parents were at church, Teresa would sneak boys into the house. Once Teresa had gone out back with one of the boys and had returned breathless, her skirt slightly twisted around her waist. Another time Raquel had lain in her bed and listened to her sister's soft laughter in the night.

Now, every evening, Raquel lay on her bed in the rented room. She studied the webs of spiders, the places where the beams didn't meet. The tiny footprints of mice on the walls.

At times Raquel was late for work because of her search for her sister, but Mrs. Randolph didn't seem to mind when Raquel arrived or when she left. Once Mrs. Randolph, who sat staring into the goldfish pond, looked up and startled Raquel when she said, "Why don't you find your sister and get yourself out of this dump?"

One morning Raquel boarded a bus that had a man playing a guitar painted on the back. It also had a small house with domestic animals. In the windows, as in all the buses, it had the names of the women the driver loved. Salsa music played when Raquel got on, and people were dancing. People always danced and sang on the buses of Panama. And a man she didn't know dropped coins into the bus driver's change box for her, in exchange for a dance.

She showed the driver the picture and he nodded. He knew the bus and he told her where to go in the city to wait for it.

Raquel was going to be late for work, but she was sure Mrs. Randolph wouldn't care, since she was probably sitting in her darkened bedroom, sipping a cool drink. She went to the place where the driver said to go, and she waited. She waited for an hour or more, and just as she was about to give up, she saw a bus approach. It pulled up like a great beast, spewing exhaust, and on the back of it she saw her sister's picture.

For a moment Raquel stared. She felt close to Teresa for the first time in three years. She felt her sister's dark eyes, looking at her from the back of the bus. When the bus began to pull away, Raquel yelled for the driver to wait. It was an early-morning bus filled with workers on their way to the hotels, to the Canal, to construction sites. The driver was old, with tired brown eyes, and he had crucifixes and statues of the Virgin on his dashboard.

When Raquel showed him the picture, he shook his head. He said he'd never seen her before. Except on the back of his bus. But he told her where to find the bus dream man. The dream man's name was Jorge and he didn't live in a good part of the city. But the driver told her how to get there and he told her to go in the heat of the day. He told her that the bus dream men were strange and filthy and he cautioned her to take care.

In the middle of the day Raquel left Mrs. Randolph and went to the slums in the old French quarter where the bus driver had told her to go. In this part of town the houses had been condemned long ago, but the poor just moved into the empty rooms. Four or five families lived in a room that had once been occupied by one. Raquel knocked on the molding where there'd once been a door. A man with greasy hair and no teeth came to her, and Raquel said, "Excuse me, but I'm looking for my sister."

The bus dream man smiled and said, "I just paint buses. I don't know many women." Raquel held out the photograph she'd been carrying for weeks. The man named Jorge touched it with his dirty hands. He smiled again through his rotten teeth and said it had been a mere coincidence.

He told Raquel how a bus driver had come to him with his new bus and he'd described a woman to him. "He told me," Jorge said, "she had eyes like the evening skies and hair as thick and dark as the forests. Skin smooth as stones on the beach. Her mouth was a cave at the bottom of the sea and her scent like the wind through the jasmine trees. Her body was the Isthmus, wide in some places, narrow in others, winding with many curves and treacherous places. A body whose distance you travel in no time, but it is a journey like the trip through the Canal that must be undertaken with great care." He said that he painted the woman the bus driver described and it happened to come out like Raquel's sister.

Raquel stood for a moment, thinking. Then she said, "You are telling me a lie." She clenched her fists, and her small, tight mouth spoke very clearly. "You know where my sister is. You can't just paint a picture like that."

The bus dream man shrugged. "I just do what I imagine. People have their wishes and dreams, their secret longings. I reveal them. That's all I do."

Raquel moved closer to him so that her face was up against his. He stank of paint and sweat and his hair was matted on his head. But he had dark, translucent eyes and he stared straight into hers. "Tell me where she is."

He smiled again. "Living out her life's dream."

The next day and the day after that Raquel left Mrs. Randolph sitting in her darkened room or counting the gold-

fish in the pond. She went and sat at the door of the bus
dream man. She watched him as he worked. He was
painting a huge bus in his backyard and he was painting
the back with a house by a lake with six children in the
lake for a man whose three children had each died at the
age of three months and who had had no more.

On the third day, when Raquel was going to leave, Mrs.
Randolph said to her, "What are you going to do when
you find your sister?"

Raquel looked at her in surprise. "I'm going to take her
home."

Mrs. Randolph shook her head of hair, which she dyed
different shades of red and yellow. "Now it's too late. She
won't go with you," Mrs. Randolph said. "Girls, when they
come to this city and stay this long, they never leave." Then
Mrs. Randolph sighed. "I had a dream last night. I dreamed
I saw bones walking by the sea. They were beautiful and
white like porcelain and they had flowers growing out of
them. But slowly veins appeared, then blood, and it was a
horrible body. Then skin. And for an instant, I saw my
daughter again. My little girl. I hadn't seen her in so many
years. I wanted to reach out and touch her . . . If I were
you, I'd go home now." Then she added as Raquel headed
to the door, "That's what I'd do if I could."

But Raquel went back to the bus dream man that day
and the days that followed. She sat without speaking as he
painted the children on the back of the bus. And finally he
turned to her and said, "All right, you win. I'll tell you
where to find her."

The Crossroads of the World Club was located at the edge
of the Zona, just below the hill where Raquel worked. She
walked by it every day as she headed up the hill to the
Randolphs'. It was a fairly well-known club, to those who
knew about such things. It was run by a man named Ed-

die, an ex-Marine, who'd once swum the Canal and had been charged a quarter for his cargo potential. It was a famous story about the Canal, and they say that Eddie, after he swam it, could never leave.

Jorge told Raquel to find Eddie. He'd told her that Eddie would tell her where her sister was. "Has she gone to America?" Raquel asked, and Jorge had smiled that same smile. "You might say she's gone to America."

Raquel hesitated before entering the club. She looked up at the Zona, so green and beautiful. Parakeets flew overhead. She heard them screeching, but she couldn't see them. She looked at the American flag she passed every day and at the Marine who guarded the entrance to the Zona. He smiled at her, the way he did every day, but he looked at her strangely when he saw her hesitating at the club.

It had no windows. There were no windows on any of the floors above it, either. Raquel had never known a building that had no windows. Even in her town in the poor houses where no breeze blew there were windows. On the outside there were pictures of dark-skinned girls and a sign that read AMERICAN SERVICEMEN WELCOME.

As her eyes adjusted to the darkness, Raquel noticed the smells of the bar. It smelled of stale flowers and darkness and of the bodies of men. Raquel didn't know the bodies of men, but when she entered the bar, she knew. It wasn't a smell like her father's or brothers' or the boy with the mustache who waited for her at home. This was a bitter smell, strong but not entirely unappealing. At night back in the Interior, Raquel had sometimes wondered about the bodies of men, wondered how she'd know them in the dark, but now she thought she'd just know.

When she could see in the darkness, she saw a bar with several men at it and a few women in the back. At the bar she asked for Eddie, and the bartender looked her over.

"You want work?"

She shook her head. "I'm working," she replied. "I want to find somebody."

The bartender shrugged and gave a call. A large burly man appeared from the back and he held out his hand to her. "I'm Eddie," he said. "What can I do for you?" She held out the photo and told him how the bus dream man had sent her here.

Eddie looked at the picture and smiled. Then he paused and stared at her. "I can see the resemblance." Raquel looked away. She'd never been the pretty one. "She'll be here tomorrow," he told her. "Come back then."

But the next day was a holiday and Raquel didn't know it. She was on her way to the club and to her job in the Zona when she got caught up in a procession. It was the day the people were carrying the bones of their leader who had died in a helicopter crash into the Canal Zone. They'd dug up his grave and they were marching, thousands of them, with his bones into the Zona. They carried banners with his words: "I don't want to go into history. I want to go into the Canal Zone." As Raquel walked, she got caught up in the crowds and they carried her along. She followed them as they wound their way up the green hill where the servicemen lived. She followed them as they proceeded past Colonel Randolph's house, where she saw the colonel and his wife, sitting on the porch, staring at the procession with the leader's bones.

At the Randolphs' house, Raquel left the procession, but neither the colonel nor his wife greeted her. When she went inside to begin her work, the colonel followed her in. He said to her, "We built it. We should keep it." And Raquel nodded and said, yes, they should keep it. But he went on. He said, "But we're going to give it back to you. We're going to give it back and watch the whole country go down the tubes." The colonel was a very tall, strong man, with his hair clipped short against his head. He reminded Raquel of a cartoon she'd once seen of Popeye the Sailor Man. Now he looked ridiculous, all puffed up and red.

Mrs. Randolph came in and sat by the pond. She glanced at Raquel and her husband, then looked at the goldfish. Her husband said something to her in English and Mrs. Randolph shrugged. She replied in Spanish, "Do what you want."

When Raquel finished her day's work, Mrs. Randolph thrust a fistful of money, all in dollars, into Raquel's hands. "Go home," Mrs. Randolph said. "Or I'll see your bones walking by the sea." And she gave her a white blouse that Raquel had admired and she told her, "Now find Teresa and promise me you'll go home."

It was the late afternoon when Raquel waved to the Marine who guarded the Zona, and she felt his eyes on her as she walked into the Crossroads of the World. It was dark inside and it took Raquel's eyes a few moments to adjust to the dark. The bar was filled with servicemen in uniform and sailors on shore leave, waiting for their ships to make the journey through the Canal.

And there were women. She saw many women sitting in the rear. They all had thick black hair and high-pitched laughs. They wore tight dresses and, from the back, they all looked the same. From the back Raquel couldn't tell one from the other. But as she approached, she heard one laugh that seemed to rise above the others.

A head turned slightly in her direction. Raquel saw a woman with eyes painted like parrot eyes and lips red as a sun rising on the Atlantic and setting on the Pacific. Her skin was smooth as stones on the shore, and the scent of jasmine rose from her body. Her body was winding and treacherous as the Isthmus. It was just as the bus dream man had said. It was what Raquel expected and what she knew she'd find. For an instant, their eyes met. Then that was all.

When Raquel left the bar, the procession was gone, and it was quiet. It was very quiet. The Marine smiled at her, and she waved faintly at him. She looked up at the hill and over to the Canal. A flock of parakeets circled overhead, screeching, flying through the palm fronds of the Zona. Raquel watched them dip and swirl and shriek as they traveled back and forth across the Canal. She decided she would go home and tell her father he should be proud. She would tell him that Teresa had made it into pictures.

Orphans of the Storm

I HAVE A SISTER named Alice who's only eight months older than I am. The reason for this eludes most people. My parents adopted Alice before they figured out my mother was already pregnant with me. And people, when they hear we're sisters, say, "Oh yes, you look just alike. Around the eyes." Alice and I don't look anything alike. She is a tall, buxom redhead and the rest of us are tiny brunettes. Alice has always stood out in a crowd.

On holidays, I usually don't have any place to go. Our parents retired to a desert community in the southwest, so I go to Alice's house. It is a standing invitation and I only have to call if I'm not coming. It has been this way ever since Alice married Jim. Actually Jim says he was hooked by Alice, but this isn't true. She simply told him he had two years from the day she finished college to decide if he was going to marry her. When the date rolled around, Alice told Jim she loved him but it was over. For a month she wouldn't see him or speak to him on the phone. Then he proposed.

Alice tells me I need a strategy with men. Every once in

a while, when something doesn't work out for me, I wind up on Alice's doorstep, and she always takes me in.

A few days before Christmas I call Alice to say I'm coming. Normally this isn't necessary, but originally I'd called to say I wasn't. The man I've been seeing on and off this past year decided at the last minute to go skiing in Colorado. I don't really understand the reasons, and Alice doesn't ask questions.

It is snowing when the train pulls in. On the train an old man sits in front of me. He has two paper bags filled with gifts, all wrapped in a sloppy way, with dirty bows stuck on. The man seems confused and keeps asking me if we've reached Wilmette. When we get to Wilmette, he gets off and wanders away into the snow.

I want to see if someone is there to meet him, but Alice comes up and hugs me, and the old man is gone. Alice never hugs me very hard. In fact I've always thought, since I was old enough to think such things, that Alice's hug feels more as if she's pushing me away. She has a sharp, angular jaw and I can feel it press sharply against my cheek.

I didn't always love Alice, but one day I suddenly did. We were walking down a street together in Oak Park and a tall, red-haired woman who looked just like Alice walked right by us. Alice looked at the woman and the woman looked at her. The woman paused, hesitated, started to speak. But Alice just grabbed my hand and quickly walked away with me. Alice was crying by the time we got home and she told me to never tell our mother what we'd seen. It was the first time I really knew she belonged to us.

Alice lives in a big stone house with a fireplace that's always going in winter. Stockings hang from the mantel, and Alice tells me they've decided to wait and open their presents when I'm there. We walk into her house arm in arm.

She says, "So this guy's in Colorado skiing, huh?"

"I don't want to talk about it. I wasn't nuts about him, anyway."

Alice nods but doesn't comprehend the notion. She has been nuts about Jim for fifteen years. Once she told me that, to this day, whenever he touches her, she goes wild. Jim works for Sunbeam and helps develop small appliances. Alice's house is filled with these appliances. Little filter machines to clean the air. Hand vacuums. Tiny electric fans you can carry in your purse.

Alice's two redheaded children, Sara and Teddy, grab me around the ankles as I walk in. Jim leans over to kiss me. He's making breakfast. He's got eggs scrambling in the electric frying pan and bacon in the microwave and muffins in the toaster oven and coffee in the coffee-maker and juice whirring around in the blender. He is the essence of efficiency as he moves quickly from one appliance to another. "How's my little Pebble?" he asks. Pebble is an old nickname from my youth. When he began dating Alice during high school, I always went along. He called me the pebble in his shoe. Then just Pebble.

Alice reaches her face up to kiss Jim hello. She's only been gone half an hour, but they seem eager to kiss. Alice's cheeks are rosy, and a droplet of mucus hangs from the tip of her nose. Jim kisses her. Then with his finger he wipes the drop away and on to his jeans. No one has ever with his own finger wiped nasal drip from my nose.

If I think back, it is the first Christmas I've been single in ten years. It's also the first Christmas I haven't been miserable in ten years. So what is worse, I ask myself. I think maybe I should call that man in Colorado and tell him just forget it.

We flock to the living room to open the gifts. At first there seems to be some system to the opening. Teddy and Sara

sit near their presents like dogs being trained to wait for a
biscuit. First they open their stocking stuffers one at a time
and display whatever Santa gave them. Then they open all
the packages that are not from Santa, and they give Alice
the cards. Alice carefully records the name of the person
who gave the gift so that thank-you notes can be written.
Then the system falls apart and we tear open our presents.

I've given Alice a lavender sweater and a pair of lavender socks. She quickly pulls the sweater on to show me it
fits. She is radiant. I reach down to open what she's bought
me. "I don't know," she mumbles. "Maybe I should have
gotten you something more practical." But I'm already
opening my gifts. The first is my stocking stuffer. It is a
small booklet, about one inch by two, entitled *What I Know
About Men*. It is a flip book of animation and I flip the
pages, and they're all blank.

Alice and I fall over laughing. Then I open a present. It
is a paperweight with a single drop inside that Alice said
reminded her of me. And finally I get a large silver angel
to stick on my wall. A guardian angel.

After the gifts are exchanged, we begin to get ready for
dinner. We examine the silver and check the glasses.
Everything matches. In my apartment, I have three Irish
coffee glasses, two brandy snifters, four wine glasses, but
they're all different. Nothing goes together.

I look at Alice, polishing silver, raising a platter to see
her face. Though this is hard for me to admit, Alice is perfect. Her house is perfect. It is decorated with angels and
lights. And she knows all of this. Knows how to make a
list for thank-you notes, knows how to set the table for
twenty people with everything matching. How to test the
silver with her reflection.

When the table is set, Alice taps me on the arm. "Come
on," she says, "we're going somewhere." We get in the car

and drive. After a few minutes I grow impatient and want to know where we're going. Alice smiles. "I want a puppy. I want Jim to have a puppy." I say all right, so we drive to Orphans of the Storm, the kennel not far from where we grew up. The kennel where we'd had all our dogs put to sleep.

The kennel has the stench of dog droppings and Lysol. It smells of wet dog hair and slightly rancid meat. A man in a white coat takes us to the cages, where dogs yelp and jump and bang themselves into the wire. There are all kinds of dogs. I tell Alice to take a red one to go with her hair. The dogs howl and never take their eyes off us. They bark as if they've been waiting for us all along.

There are beautiful dogs with mottled coats. There's a Husky with yellow-green eyes. But Alice stops in front of the ugliest dog I've ever seen. He has a blue eye and a brown one and part of his ear has been bitten away. He is mangy and has big flat paws. He doesn't bark or jump. He follows us with his calm, steady stare. He doesn't seem to expect very much. Alice says she'll take that one, because he'll never find a home.

Everyone likes Buick immediately. That's the dog's name. Somebody found him in an abandoned Buick. But Buick is not so sure how he feels about his new home. He sulks and wags his tail tentatively. To me he appears ungrateful, but Alice says he'll come around.

Just before dinner, I go upstairs to take a shower. The bathroom is through their bedroom, and Alice has neatly laid out my towels. I take my shower, but before going into the guest room where I'm to get dressed, I open Alice's closet.

First I find bags of clothing, complete with labels: "Transitional spring and fall, except for corduroy" and "Jim's summer suits." And then inside the closet the blouses, the skirts, the suits and pants, all in their proper place. I move on to shoes. Each pair of shoes is in a box and each box has a label. Green sling-backs from Field's, suede pumps with purple flowers from Saks, Yves St. Laurent black sandals with red buckles from Paris, Maud Frizon purple shoes with spike heels. There were Docksiders and Tretorns, tennis shoes, and running shoes. Shoes from the L. L. Bean catalogue. Waders and black boots with walking heels. Frye boots, Bandolino gangster moll shoes with open toes in beige, black alligator sandals from Pappagallo, purchased near the Spanish Steps.

I move on to the drawers. I open a drawer filled with Jim's underwear, and on his socks, on each pair of his socks, is his name, carefully sewn. I open the drawer of the night table with the Sunbeam electric blanket dial and find spermicide, an applicator, a diaphragm case, all in a little box. I close the drawer quickly when I hear footsteps enter the room.

Jim comes in and sees me standing in my towel, his closets and drawers opened. "You lost?"

"I was looking for a robe."

"Oh." He flings one at me, which I awkwardly slip on over my towel. "You staying for the weekend?"

I shake my head. "I've got a lot of work to do."

Jim sits down at the edge of the bed. "You're never going to meet a guy, working so hard." Actually I don't work very hard, but I'm always on call. I work for a man who makes commercials. I'm the one who makes soap bubble, beer foam. I've been flown to Los Angeles to squeeze a tube of toothpaste.

"I've got a date tomorrow night." I blush in defense of myself. "To go ice-skating." Jim nods. "With an accountant." Jim smiles.

"Anything serious?" I shake my head. "Well, I hope it will be soon." He sighs wistfully as he walks toward the door. "Nothing like it when it is."

For dinner Alice has a turkey and a goose and two kinds of stuffing. She has sweet potatoes and cranberry sauce and creamed spinach and three pies and I don't know what else. Just before the guests arrive, Jim begins to carve. He puts a fork firmly into the turkey's back and brings the knife gently to the side. He brings the knife back and forth again while Alice holds out a platter. He carves smoothly and well and puts the meat carefully onto the platter that Alice is holding. They have worked up this act. I watch as he brings the knife back and I can picture him in the act of love, moving with an even, steady motion.

Once when we were in college and I visited Alice, we all slept in the same room and I watched them making love. They thought I was asleep and Jim kept saying to Alice, over and over, "Is this all right? Do you like this?" And Alice said, "Shush, I'll die if you wake Jennie." But I'd been awake the entire time and I'd watched the way their bodies moved, with Alice's beautiful red hair flowing off the bed.

The next night I go out with the accountant. We go to an outdoor skating rink and drink Irish coffees. During an Irish coffee, he says he knows if he's going to fall in love with a girl after talking to her for fifteen seconds. Since he and I have been talking for a few hours already, it doesn't seem that I'm a likely candidate. He takes me home, rolls a joint, and we make love foolishly. After he leaves, I think about Alice. How she has it all.

A few days later I go to a department store and buy sheets. My mother bought some sheets for me when I graduated from college, and I've been sleeping in them ever since. Suddenly I can't stand the lack of texture. The way they feel all polished like smooth stones.

I've never bought sheets before. Not for myself. I've bought other things since I graduated from college. Cross-country skis and dresses for parties and trips to the south.

But sheets and dishes and nightgowns, those things I bought
for other people. For people who were going to be married. But suddenly I have to go and make those purchases.

The department store confuses me at first, so I go di-
rectly to the linens section. There's a white sale and I watch
the women as they pick up the packages and squeeze them,
as if they're buying cantaloupe. A salesgirl, seeing me bewildered, comes up and offers to help. She's young, with
very white teeth and blond hair that looks dyed. I tell her
I want sheets for regular occasions, and sheets for special
occasions. She gives me a knowing smile.

I buy bags full of purple and white flowered sheets. I buy
beige sheets with lace sidings, a purple and white com-
forter cover, and four down pillows. I spend more money
on my sheets than I've ever spent on anything. Then I go
home and make my bed. I put on the new and toss out the
old. It is a Saturday night, so I go down the street and buy
a newspaper. Then, even though it is early in the evening,
I crawl into my bed. I can hear all kinds of sounds outside. Drunk people wandering home from parties, people
having fights. Car doors opening, slamming shut. I open
the paper and begin to read. The new sheets feel different
from the old ones. They are crisp and they scratch a little
as I try to sleep.

I call Alice on her birthday and say I want to come out
and see her. She says there isn't going to be much of a party
this year, just a few old friends are stopping by, but I can
come if I want. She sounds distracted, and I can hear Sara
crying. When I get to her house, it's quiet and doesn't feel
as though she's going to have a party. The house isn't decorated with balloons and paper streamers, and I can't find
any chicken salad in the icebox. Buick lies lethargically in
a corner, ignoring us all.

Alice sits at the kitchen table for a few moments, sipping coffee. Then she asks me if I want to come down to

the basement and help her with the laundry. I find it a little odd that Alice is doing the laundry on her birthday, when she's having a few friends over, but I don't see any reason not to help her.

We go downstairs; the basement is damp and cold. She has a washer and dryer and there are piles of laundry on the floor. There seems to be a ton of laundry. I've never seen so much clothing. There are sheets and towels and socks and gym clothes all mixed together. Colors lie with whites. And to one side there are more baskets of clothes. There are so many shirts and socks. They look as if they belong to a man. Alice picks up a handful. "These are Jim's," she says to me. I nod. I tell her I know. Plaid shirts and green pants. Sweats and a man's undershirt. She picks up a handful and stuffs them into my face. "Smell them," she says.

"What?" I step back in surprise.

"Go on," she says, "smell them."

I smell them. They smell like a man's body. Like a man's sweat. And they smell like something else, but I can't figure it out. "They smell dirty," I say.

But Alice shakes her head. "Don't you smell anything else?" This time she separates some underwear from the rest of his clothes. She takes some underpants and shirts and stuffs these in my face. I breathe in deeply.

"They smell nice," I say dumbly.

"Perfume," Alice says. "French perfume, I think."

I nod, sniffing Jim's underpants, which she holds up to my nose. "Smells good."

She stuffs them into the washing machine. "I don't wear perfume." She puts in a plaid shirt with his underwear. "I'm allergic to it. My skin breaks out in hives." Alice takes a very large amount of soap and dumps it into the washing machine. "If I just put a tiny dot on my skin, I get a big blotch."

"Oh," I say. And then add, "I never knew that."

"That's why Mom never gives me perfume. When we were little and Mom would dab some on me, I'd break out. I think I react to the stuff that comes from whales. Maybe they don't get it from whales anymore. But I haven't tried it. I'm probably not allergic to the synthetic thing they use. Anyway, the cause doesn't matter. What matters is I don't use perfume. I never have."

She bangs the door of the washer shut and begins removing things from the dryer. She takes out shirts and socks and puts them on top of the large folding table. She folds them and puts them in a basket. "When you live in a house for as long as I've lived in this, you get to know the way it smells," Alice tells me. "I know when things are burning. I know when the cats piss on the rug." I help her fold.

"I washed everything," she goes on. "I must've washed everything in his closet a dozen times. I wanted to get rid of the smell and I wanted them to be clean before I packed them. I've packed most of them. This is all that's left."

Alice begins to match some of his socks. "I even know who she is. She designs the little appliances. You know, the miniature electric fan; that was her brainstorm."

During her birthday party, Alice runs up and down the stairs with Jim's fresh laundry. Alice is normal with Jim. She hangs on his arm. Kisses him on the cheek. He keeps his arm tightly around her. And then after the party, when the guests are leaving, Jim goes to take his elderly aunt home. While he is gone, Alice and I put all of Jim's things into several suitcases. "Alice," I say, "are you sure about this? I mean, shouldn't you think it out?"

Alice looks at me with a strange smile. "Don't you think I already have?" She takes a tag and puts it on one of the suitcases. We lug them out into the driveway and place them right where Jim would run over them when he comes into the drive. The tag says, "Don't bother coming in." After we do that, we start to make dinner. We use all of Jim's appliances, every single one.

While we are making dinner, Jim pulls into the driveway. The car screeches to a halt; the door slams. We go to the window and see Jim, staring at his luggage. Alice turns away, but I watch him hurling the suitcases into the car.

That night I sleep in the back bedroom with Sara. I am tired, but for some reason I wake in the middle of the night. It is a bright moonlit night and the moonlight makes the snow a very silvery blue. In the snow, I see Alice, walking Buick. She has him on a very long lead and she is walking him across the snow. I think how beautiful it is, to see Alice walking Buick in the moonlight in the snow.

But then I think how it's rather late to be walking a dog. And the dog doesn't seem to want to be walked at all. In fact, I can see the mark of his whole body in the snow, where he's being dragged. Buick is a fairly large dog and it's not easy to drag him, so Alice must really be much stronger than she looks.

I watch for a few moments from the window to see where she's dragging him. She drags him to a tree that grows close to the ground in the backyard. I see her get to the tree and toss the lead over a branch. She tugs on the rope and Buick rises, struggling and making a kind of yelping noise, off the ground, those big, flat paws clawing at the air.

I run downstairs and pull on a pair of galoshes. In my nightgown, the cold slapping my skin, I run out across the snow, shouting at Alice. I don't know what I'm saying, but I feel the impact of my body as it hits hers, like a football player in a fierce tackle. We sail into the snow, and Buick goes yelping off across the yard. We are both in nightgowns, the snow goes right to our skin. Our nightgowns lift up, and in the cold snow our bodies come together. Alice rolls on top of me and tries to smash my head into the snow. I turn her over and hold her down.

Alice shouts at me how he's a mean, nasty dog and she'll just have to give him back to the kennel. She says how they'll just put him to sleep. I press my arms on her wrists, my knees into her legs. I feel the warmth of her thighs against my thighs in the snow. It is a strange feeling, for we are both hot and cold at the same time. "I hate you," I tell her. "I always have."

After I say it, I let her go. I get up and shake the snow off me. She shakes the snow off herself. We stand there together, shivering. For a moment we stare at each other. "I didn't mean that," I say. "I just always thought you had it all." And then she grabs me. I think she is going to strangle me too and I struggle to get away, but instead she presses me to her and sobs. I hold Alice, broken, cold as winter, whiskey-breathed, with snot drops frozen to her nostrils. I lift up the hem of my nightgown and bring it to her face.

I take her upstairs and we put on dry nightgowns. I crawl into bed and wrap my arms around her. The dog curls foolishly on the floor, his memory obliterated. The moon shines a path into the room, and outside I see the snow. It is that midwestern winter I know so well. Pristine, all just right, the moonlight, the crackling noises, the snow crashing from the trees and sounding like the footsteps of small animals traveling across the roof. From the bed I see icicles hanging from the roof. I want to break one off and suck on it, but Alice is falling asleep in my arms.

The Typewriter

ON THE NIGHT TRAIN to Venice, Bill and Clara had a compartment to themselves. They locked the door and pulled down the shades. They opened a bottle of wine and ate ham and cheese sandwiches. Clara lay with her head in Bill's lap, reading out loud from the guidebook, while Bill ran his fingers through her hair as if he were sifting sand. They were tired from the three days they'd spent in Paris, so when the porter came in to make up their berths, Bill yawned and put the typewriter on the overhead rack. He slipped it in his jacket, wrapping the sleeves around the body of the typewriter. "I don't want somebody coming in here in the night and stealing it."

It surprised Clara that for a little while she had forgotten about the typewriter. Perhaps, she thought, she'd forget about it altogether. They brushed their teeth in the tiny sink in their compartment. Then Bill kissed her good night and climbed into the upper berth. For a few moments Clara lay on her back in the lower berth, listening to the rhythmic clacking of the wheels, to the sound of the train whizzing across France.

She reached her hand so that it curled around the rail of Bill's berth, and Bill played with her fingertips for a while until she scurried up the ladder into the narrow bunk beside him. "Hi."

"Hi." He moved nearer the wall, but his eyes stayed closed. "You wanta snuggle?" He tucked her in the space of his arm, but said no more. Clara looked over and saw Bill's jacket, wrapped around the typewriter. She looked away. "Can we go to San Marco tomorrow?" she whispered in his ear, as if she didn't want to be overheard.

"We can do whatever you want."

"Maybe three days won't be enough there."

"Honey" — he kissed her on the forehead — "I don't think I'm over my jet lag. Can we talk in the morning?" She huddled closer but felt cramped.

"Sure, we can talk in the morning."

Clara went back to her berth, but she stared out the window for a long time. The typewriter rattled back and forth in the overhead rack like a restless person trying to sleep, and she wished Bill were awake, reading the guidebook with her, so that she could forget about it again. Ten days before they left on this vacation, Bill had told her not to get upset, but he was going to bring a typewriter along. Clara didn't get upset. She'd just inquired, "Does that mean you plan to work? On our vacation?"

Bill, a reporter for a Los Angeles newspaper, had shaken his head. He told her the typewriter wasn't for him. It was for an old friend of his family. "She's going blind and she wants to write, so my mother asked me if we'd take her a typewriter." Bill told Clara her name was Madame Estella and she lived on an island off Greece.

For ten days Clara had tried not to dwell on the typewriter, but something about it bothered her. Clara made a lot of money writing scripts for movies that never got made. She was starting to feel like a failure, so they'd decided to take some time off and go on a vacation. For six weeks they had planned not to plan their vacation. They were going to travel without an itinerary. They'd start in France and end up in Spain, but that was all they knew. Their luggage, packed weeks in advance, consisted of two backpacks.

Finally one night Clara had got up the nerve and said to Bill, "Darling, what if we don't want to go to Greece? What if we want to go to Sweden?"

But he'd replied, "How could anyone not want to go to Greece." She'd told him that wasn't the point, and Bill had stared at her. They rarely fought, but that night they did. Clara told him he put everybody else before her, or at least she felt that he did. Bill said he didn't. Then she found herself reminding him of the night when they were just starting to make love and his ex-wife, Patti, called. Her brakes had failed on the coast road and she needed a tow getting out of the sand dune, so Bill went right over to her. "You could have said no to Patti that night, couldn't you? You could have told her to call a tow truck or that actor she'd been seeing."

Bill had defended himself. "Patti doesn't make the kind of money you do, and the actor was on location somewhere. There wasn't anyone else she could call." His face had reddened as he'd argued with her. He didn't like to argue. "I suppose I could have told her to call a tow truck," he said finally, for the sake of harmony. "But this is different." He just wanted to bring a typewriter to a poor old woman who was going blind and couldn't afford to buy one for herself.

At last Clara admitted her problem to him. "Having a typewriter with us will only remind me of what a flop I am."

And he'd kissed her. "Oh, darling, you aren't a flop." She had wanted to discuss in greater detail how she felt,

but for Bill the problem was solved. "Don't worry." He'd
kissed her on the cheek. "I'll carry it."

The next morning in Venice they went for a long gondola
ride and saved a pigeon that was drowning in the canal.
They walked through a huge palace and made love fiercely
before dinner. After they made love, Clara pointed to the
typewriter. "I want to look at it," she said. They'd had it
with them for almost a week, but she'd never looked at it.
Bill put the case on the desk and Clara opened it. Inside
sat a small Olivetti manual. It was ordinary enough. It was
brown, the color of mud and excrement. She closed it
quickly.

As they walked along the canals, heading to a seafood
restaurant, Clara complained that the things she wrote never
got made into movies and that she hated L.A. "But," she
went on, "I make so much money. It's not easy to give it
all up."

Bill held her hand, trying to act as if he hadn't heard her
talk about this a hundred times before. "But you've got
talent. You could do something besides disaster films and
episodes of 'Life with Lily.' "

She stared at him, wide-eyed. "You really think so?"

On a little bridge he kissed her as a gondola sailed by.
"I'm sure of it."

When they got to the restaurant, he hoped she'd drop
it, but as soon as they sat down, Clara said, "Can we talk
about the typewriter?"

Bill felt his stomach tightening. He watched her sitting
there. She wasn't the prettiest woman he'd ever been with.
Patti was a knockout, but he'd been struck by Clara right
away. Her green eyes, her salt and pepper hair, her smooth
skin, had enchanted him two years ago when they met at
the beach bar. But she was driving him nuts with the way
she dwelled for days on some insignificant thing, to the

point where she could think of nothing else. "You always need to talk about things. Let's have a nice dinner?"

"Look," she said, "I understand why you brought it. I understand that that poor old woman needs it. I only want to explain to you how I feel." Clara knew something was wrong, but she couldn't quite put her finger on it. "I feel like a failing law student taking a trip with all her law books. As if I have to study all the time. As if it's reminding me of how badly I'm doing. I'd wanted to get away on this trip. And now we're traveling with that stupid typewriter."

Bill didn't think the law student simile was very good. Maybe she was a flop, as she said. "You've got only one problem." He patted her hand. "You dwell on stuff too much." They walked back to the hotel without saying more, but when they got in their room, he held her. She felt safe. She knew that this was his way. This, she knew, was the best he could do. In bed, he made her forget whatever had been on her mind.

In the morning Bill woke to the sound of the typewriter. He was a heavy sleeper and could sleep through almost anything, but the typing went on for so long that he was finally aroused. He opened his eyes and saw Clara, hair disheveled, in a cotton nightie, pecking away. "What're you doing?"

"I've got an idea." She didn't pause from her typing. "For a screenplay. It's about two people on vacation."

"Oh . . ." He watched her breasts bounce as she wrote. He got up and kissed her on the back of the neck. "Come on. Let's get some breakfast."

"Why don't you go without me?" Clara said. "I want to work on this."

"Clara, we're in Venice. You can type any time." But she was adamant, so Bill went down to San Marco without her. He ate a roll and drank two cups of coffee. He walked along the Grand Canal and bought postcards. He sent his mother a card of a little boy covered with pigeons. He sent Patti a card of a nighttime gondola ride and said he'd never felt better. On the back of a picture of Venice under water, he wrote his best friend that he was thinking of coming home early. Then he went to a museum and looked at frescoes he didn't understand.

He went to American Express and purchased two first-class tickets on a boat the next afternoon for the coast of Yugoslavia. He would surprise her. When he got back to the hotel, Clara still was typing. He showed her the tickets. She said she wasn't sure she wanted to leave Venice. She had a lot of work to do.

He managed to get her packed and onto the ship. He folded the pages she'd written and put them into a pocket of his backpack. They had a lovely cabin with a queen-size bed and a porthole. Together they watched the yellow lights of Italy disappear. Then they closed the porthole and made love as the ship rocked back and forth.

In the morning Bill found Clara reading the pages she'd written in Venice. She'd dug them out of his backpack while he slept. "Can I read what you wrote?" he asked. Clara handed him the pages. The piece was called "The Journey," and it was about twenty pages of their trip thus far. It wasn't very good. "Do you like it?" Clara asked.

"It's very interesting."

She knew he was lying. "What's wrong with it?" Bill picked at some lint on the covers. "If you don't like it, can't you say why?" He kept picking at the covers, so Clara took the pages from him and tore them up. Then she opened the porthole and tossed them into the Adriatic near the shores of Yugoslavia.

They didn't say a word to each other during the drive along the Dalmatian Coast. Bill wrote in his journal and

Clara stared blankly out the bus at the turquoise waters of the sea. The bus was hot and she tried to open a window, but the man behind her pulled it shut. Another man in the back of the bus smiled at her and motioned for them to change seats with him. He put his hand over his heart, then shaped his hands into a pleading sign.

Clara traded seats with the deaf mute because he insisted. He wrote his name, Piro, on a piece of paper. When the bus made a pit stop, Clara, Bill, and Piro went to have a cup of coffee. Piro talked to Clara with his hands. He told her he had two wives and five children. One of the children was also a deaf mute. He told her he had divorced one wife because she nagged him. The divorced wife lived in a city to the north. He told her he had a house in the woods and worked as a blacksmith. He liked Americans and he wanted to travel to America someday. He wrote his address on the piece of paper with his name on it and asked them to send him a postcard from New York. He asked Clara if he could find work in America as a blacksmith and Clara told him he could.

When the bus reached Dubrovnik, Clara finally spoke to Bill. She said to him, "I can find more things to say to a Serbo-Croatian deaf mute than I can find to say to you."

They spent Easter in Crete. They wanted to see how the real Cretans lived, so they asked around and someone told them about a little town on the west shore. But the bus, they were told, stopped three miles from the town. So they hired a cab and figured they'd find a way out when the time came.

The drive from the main road to Bahia was steep and dusty. As they came closer, Clara's heart sank. The little village was dotted with slums and construction sites. Dust and garbage littered the side of the road. It wasn't what they'd had in mind. The town had no hotels, so they checked into a guest house that was on the water. Their room was dirty and filled with cobwebs and the smell of mildew.

On their way to the beach, they stopped in the souvenir shop to buy postcards and suntan lotion. The man who ran the shop spoke a broken English. His in-laws ran the guest house where Bill and Clara were staying. His wife had gone for the day with his son to a nearby town.

Clara leaned forward. "How'd she get there?"

"She took our car," the man told her.

"Oh," Clara replied, and she asked him very politely if he would consider driving them back to the main road when they were ready to leave the town. The man said he would drive them. Clara smiled at Bill as she walked ahead of him. "See? I told you we'd get a ride."

They descended the hill to the beach and saw that everyone was naked. Bill hesitated, but Clara said, "Come on, don't be so uptight." Clara took off her suit right away and ran to the water while Bill waded slowly toward her. She tried to pull off his suit when he got near, but he swam away to a rock about a hundred yards out to sea. Clara swam after him to the rock, and when they reached it, Bill took off his suit, tossed it onto the rock.

The water was very cool, and Bill felt the cold water moving between his thighs. He put his hands around her waist. He thought how perfect it all was. How simple things could be. Here he was, naked, treading water in the Aegean, with his hands wrapped gently around Clara's waist.

Clara pressed her body against his. She tried to move his hands up to her breasts. Bill didn't know how to explain it to her. He felt closer to her with his hands resting on her waist. He felt closer just holding her hand as they swam. "No," he muttered, taking his hands away, "I don't want to." He didn't mean to sound so abrupt. "I just want to swim around," he added gently.

"You never want to," Clara said as she swam to shore.
That night they got drunk on ouzo. Bill passed out as
soon as his head hit the pillow, but Clara tossed in damp
sheets and swatted mosquitoes. She thought that there was
something about him that he always kept to himself, some
part of him she could never reach. She looked at him
sleeping, his back to her, and felt alone. She got up and
saw the moon over the Aegean.

She decided to work on the story she'd begun about the
two people on a journey. She tried to begin in Paris, but
she found herself writing about the night when she and Bill
were going to make love and Patti called to say her brakes
had failed on the coast road. She was writing that Bill had
shuffled his feet and turned away from her when he spoke
on the phone so that she couldn't see his face.

She tried to get the typewriter back to the story of the
two people on vacation, but it wouldn't go back. It followed Bill as his eyes glanced at her, then back at the phone,
as he dressed slowly, methodically tying his shoelaces. It
followed him as he walked to the door, as he kissed her
on the cheek, then waved sheepishly from his car. The
typewriter described Clara standing at the door, naked, the
breeze from the Pacific blowing in as she'd watched him
drive away.

The next day as Bill held Clara's breasts up in the water,
she decided to ask him if anything had happened that night
when Patti's car broke down. She was about to ask when
he banged his foot into a rock. She counted twenty-three
sharp black spines embedded in his heel. While Bill hob-
bled back to the guest house, Clara wandered through town,
trying to find first-aid cream, but she couldn't find any.
When she got back, their landlady, her hair wrapped in a
bandanna, was frying fish.

"Excuse me," Clara said. She pointed to her heel, then

pointed upstairs. The woman nodded. She had seen Bill
hobble in. Then Clara made sharp staccato jabs with her
index finger into her palm. The woman nodded again and
laughed. Clara understood that this must happen often to
tourists. Then Clara made a sewing gesture and the landlady went into a box and handed Clara a needle.

As Clara headed up the stairs, the woman caught her by
the arm. She had a round face and bright blue eyes. She
smiled, pointed to her crotch, and then to Clara's foot. Then
she said, "Psss." Clara watched as the woman made a long
stream of water with her hands.

"Psss?" Clara repeated out loud. The woman nodded,
laughed, and went back to her fish.

Bill was examining his foot when Clara got upstairs. The
spines were hurting and the heel was beginning to swell.
Clara passed the needle through a match flame. "The
woman who runs this place told me to piss on your foot."

Bill looked stunned. "Why, for Christ's sake?"

"I guess it's supposed to take the spines out." She turned
his foot over. She picked the few spines that were on the
surface with the needle.

Bill shook his head. "Uric acid? You think it would
work?"

Clara laughed. "I don't know, but I'm not pissing on your
foot."

In the morning Bill's foot was puffed up and an odd shade
of gray. He could hardly put his shoe on. Clara was worried. "You should see a doctor."

She ran over to the souvenir shop and told the man there
that they needed a ride as soon as possible to the main road.
He seemed annoyed but said he'd be over in half an hour.
While Clara packed, Bill sat downstairs on the porch,
waiting for the man. Finally he came by. He told Bill he
was sorry, but he was out of gas. Bill looked at his pack,
at the typewriter. "All right," he said to the man, "thanks
anyway."

When Clara came down with her pack, Bill told her that the man from the souvenir shop was out of gas. Clara didn't believe the story. "Didn't you argue with him?" She looked at the dirt road, twisting up the mountain to the main road.

"He said he was out of gas." Bill pulled on his pack and grimaced. He picked up the typewriter.

Clara strapped on her pack. "He lied to you," she said. "Don't you know when somebody is lying to you?" Bill started walking. "It's a three-mile walk out of here," she called out to him. "Here, let me take it." She reached to take the typewriter from his hand, but he walked ahead, trying not to limp.

"I said I'd carry it," he shouted as he moved up the road. "And I will."

They missed the three o'clock bus and got to Heraklion late. They checked into a pension, and while Bill soaked his foot, Clara said gently, "Tell me, that night when Patti called, you were gone a long time."

Bill was concentrating on trying to squeeze one of the spines out of his heel.

"Is there anything you want to tell me?" Clara asked. "Did anything happen?" Bill's eyes flitted back and forth. He said nothing, so Clara continued, "If something happened, it's all right. I mean, it's not completely all right, but you two were together a long time and those things can happen. But do you want to tell me about it?"

Bill looked up, a wide smile on his lips. "Who puts such things in your head? You should save them for your scripts."

"I'd feel better if you told me."

But Bill just shook his head. "Save your crazy ideas for your scripts."

When Bill got in bed, Clara began a letter, explaining why she was leaving him. She told him how he'd grown so remote, so detached, how they didn't share things anymore. Clara began to tell him that it didn't really matter if something had happened that night with Patti; what mattered was he wouldn't talk to her about it. She paused to think, but now the typewriter typed on its own. She watched as its keys clacked away without her fingers touching them. Terrified, not knowing what to do, Clara put her hands back on the keys, and her hands followed the typewriter. It told how Patti's car hadn't broken down at all. It told how she'd just pleaded with him to come over, how they'd made love on her living room floor.

Clara stopped, leaned back in her chair, but the type-writer kept going. It told her things she didn't remember. About a Sunday afternoon when she was a girl and her parents were barbecuing in the backyard. While Clara set the picnic table, her father, spatula in hand, said, "Don't put the napkin on the right. It goes on the left." Her mother, carrying the potato salad, came outside. She let the screen door slam as she glared at Clara's father. "Let her do it the way she wants." Her mother plunked the potato salad down. "You think your way is the only way." The type-writer said it was the beginning of the end.

It went on. It reminded her that her mother had moved into the spare room not long after that picnic. That her father used to stand in her room in the middle of the night, just shaking his head.

When Clara tried to stop, it kept on. Her nightgown clung to her damp breasts. Her arms ached. Her hands felt as if they could drop from her wrists. Into the night she typed, and whenever she paused, the typewriter kept on. Bill put the pillow over his head, assuming Clara was working on another script that would never get made into a film.

In the morning a doctor drained the infection and re-moved the spines from Bill's foot. In the afternoon they sailed for Epheus, one of the tiniest of the Greek isles. They found a hotel and decided to go look for Madame Estella right away. They'd been told by Bill's mother that they just had to ask and they'd find her. Bill carried the typewriter. Clara said, "Maybe we could keep it. Maybe we could just buy her another one."

Bill shook his head. "I thought you were dying to get rid of this thing."

"I'm working well on it," Clara said.

"I don't think this island has a typewriter store," Bill said.

"I'd like to keep it," she said a bit more firmly.

They found the main street in town and followed the directions they'd been given. The town was stark white and bright blue, and the glare hurt their eyes. They asked a boy if he knew where Madame Estella lived, and the boy led them over broken slate and down narrow staircases. Sweat ran down Clara's neck and she tried to shade her eyes from the glare. She touched Bill's arm. "I think we should be apart for a while," she said to him simply. "I'm going on my own when we get to Athens."

Bill nodded solemnly. He too was sweating. The light hurt his eyes. "I think it's a good idea." He looked at Clara. Her hair, her eyes, her body. At that moment he thought she was very beautiful.

He didn't know what to say. He wanted to tell her how much he loved her. He wanted to tell her how glad he'd been to go home with her that first night. How much he liked lying in bed with her, just listening to the sound of the ocean outside. How that night with Patti had been an accident and he hadn't been able to be straight with her since then, but the words wouldn't come. Clara twisted her hair up off her neck. The back of her neck was soaking wet, as if they'd just finished making love. He ran his hand through the sweat and rubbed it away. She leaned against him and he pulled her close.

The boy stopped and pointed to a door. He smiled and

left them. Bill fumbled for a coin but the boy shook his head, motioning *no,* and he was gone. "I'll go back to Italy," Clara said, finishing their talk. "We can meet up in Spain."

"We're on the same flight back," Bill said.

They stared at the door where the boy had led them, glad to have finally reached their destination. It gave them something else to think about now. The door seemed to lead to a basement. They walked down two steps. Inside, it was dark and one of the panes of glass in the door was missing. They knocked several times, each time knocking louder and louder, and finally a voice called out in English, from somewhere inside, "It's open."

Bill pushed the door hesitantly and they walked in. The room was cold and very dim. The cement floor felt moist and slick under their sandals, and there was the smell of filth and decay. There was also the odor of sewage. In a corner, under a heap of covers, they could make out a form that seemed to be stirring. "Wait," they heard the voice say, "let me put on a robe."

"It's Bill Jefferies. Did you get my cable? My mom asked me to look you up," Bill called toward the bed.

"Oh, I expected you last week. Didn't you say the seventeenth?" In the darkness they saw the shape, large, white, and naked, rising up. Bill and Clara looked away. "I thought you'd be on the ferry then." They heard the shuffling of feet. "My eyes aren't very good," she mumbled. "I can't see you. What time is it?"

Out of the shadows the woman appeared. She was tall and old and she moved toward them in a bathrobe that was partly open, revealing her sagging breasts. "No, I wasn't expecting you. I don't even know what day it is."

Madame Estella reached out, groping for them. Into the light her two hands emerged. The fingers were gnarled, the knuckles swollen, the hands turned inward like birds' feet.

"I should have written back when you wrote me. But I couldn't, you see." She held up her hands. "My hands, they're useless to me."

Bill nodded. "Oh," he said.

"From the cold," she explained, dropping her hands back to her side. "I couldn't write."

Bill nodded again. Clara could not bring herself to look at him. He put the typewriter down behind him and stepped forward so that his body concealed it. Clara stood back and felt the cold enter her toes.

When they reached their guest house, she lay down for a moment. Clara made the decision in her mind to keep the typewriter. She knew it had to mean something, that the old woman couldn't use it. She knew she was supposed to keep it. She didn't mean to, but she fell asleep. When she woke up, Bill was gone. So was the typewriter. Clara ran around the room, frantically looking for it, but it wasn't anywhere.

A little later Bill came back, waving money in his hand. He'd sold the typewriter for fifty dollars to a man on his way to Turkey.

"You sold it?" Clara asked, dismayed.

Bill kissed her. "You didn't really want it, did you? I thought you'd be pleased."

They walked back to Madame Estella's to give her the money. "Poor thing," Bill said. "I'm sure she can use it." Clara moved closer to him, slipping her arm through his. "I think that's a very nice thing to do." She squeezed his arm. She thought he really was a kind man. That it was his kindness she'd loved in the first place. Bill put his arm around her and they walked in silence, both thinking it best to say nothing for a while.

The Watermelon People

MANGO JACK has been living in Honduras too long. You can see that right away. You can tell by the way the sweat clings like a crystal fixture to his receding brow and by the way he walks in the heat in his Panama shirt, lugging a suitcase, slumped like a chimpanzee. You can tell he hasn't been anywhere else in a while and that he's hungry to see Americans, because he appears on the dock in La Ceiba, where we're standing, as soon as the bus drops us off.

The dock is deserted and looks as if it hasn't been used for years. Its wood is rotting, planks missing. The smell of bananas and sewage fills the air. Two other Americans stand at the dock, a man and a woman with backpacks. She has long brown hair and pasty skin. He seems to match her. They look bewildered and smile sickly at us. We all have the same guidebook, open to the same page, to the passage that tells us that regular ferries sail to the Bay Islands from here.

Melanie tugs at my arm. "Let's look at that guidebook again," she says. Melanie is a very trusting person. What she reads in books, she believes. She's kept this page of

the guidebook dog-eared across Mexico, through Guatemala. It kept her going through Honduras. It took a lot to
get her to agree to take this trip with me. She'd wanted to
see the Grand Canyon, but I said, "You can always see
the Grand Canyon." She reads the words of the guidebook out loud, as if she's just learning the language. "Ferries leave regularly from the dock at La Ceiba . . ." She
cannot finish the passage. She looks at the dock and just
shakes her head.

That's when Mango Jack arrives. He seems to come out
of nowhere, as if he were waiting for us behind one of the
wooden posts. Even though he's carrying a large suitcase,
I'm sure he wasn't on the bus. He's an odd-looking man,
and I have no sense of his age. His face is round and pale
and he seems to have no facial hair. There's a grimness to
his features, and I immediately feel sorry for him, though
I don't know why.

"I bet you're trying to get to the Bay Islands," he says
with a short, huffy laugh, as if he's run a long way. He
wipes the sweat from his brow with a handkerchief, but
the sweat reappears as soon as the handkerchief goes back
into his pocket. "Somebody should write to those people
in England and tell them. Ferry hasn't run in years." We
nod, as if we should have known this all along. "Not many
tourists come across Honduras these days. People who go
to the Bay Islands, they fly down from San Juan."

Melanie looks at me. This isn't what she'd had in mind.
She mumbles, "You mean, we can't get to Roatán?" The
news is also starting to sink in to me. What had gotten us
through the Guatemalan jungle and the Honduran coun-
tryside was the thought of a beach.

"Oh, you can get there, all right." The couple is standing close to us now, and we all introduce ourselves. We
form a kind of football huddle around Mango Jack. He
says his real name is Teddy Jackson, but the islanders have

called him Mango Jack for as long as he can remember. Then he winks at us and says, "Just stick with me." Mango Jack has a pilot friend, and he says that for twenty dollars each we can charter his plane. He fumbles in his pocket for money and comes up with none. "Damn it," he says. "Left my checkbook on Roatán and I'm out of cash." He tells us as he lugs his suitcase to a taxi that he'll get us to the beach resort at Roatán, where his checkbook is waiting. If we front him the money, he'll be glad to help us out.

Melanie and I are happy to have someone watch over us. For a while we haven't been feeling safe. When we crossed into Guatemala, everything changed. Soldiers stopped our buses. Women hid their faces in hand-woven shawls while the men pretended to look away. Sometimes a soldier pulled a man off the bus and told the driver to drive away. The soldiers said they were looking for tax evaders and illegals, but when the soldiers left, the women wailed. From Guatemala we wanted to go into El Salvador, but the man who sold us bus tickets said the border was bad and we should stick to the tourist trail.

We headed to Copán. Near Copán we stayed in a jungle town in hammocks and at night heard the distant thumping of drums. At five in the morning a pickup truck took us to the border, and in Honduras everything changed again. The heat was terrible and we could see the air. At the border we drank Cokes and a radio played "Stayin' Alive." But there were no more checkpoints. No more soldiers to contend with.

A man got on our first bus in Honduras with his daughter. They sat in the front of the bus and after a while the father got off and waved good-bye to his daughter. She was about thirteen, and she waved to him. Then the girl began to sob. She sobbed uncontrollably, and the driver stopped the bus. Women flocked to the girl's side, then shook their heads. The driver shook his head, then drove on, with the girl sobbing. She was an idiot and her father had abandoned her on the bus. Melanie and I looked helplessly around. The man behind us said, "Too expensive to keep. Too expensive to feed."

When we got on the bus to La Ceiba, the driver asked if we were watermelon people, and everyone laughed. Melanie and I didn't understand. So he asked again, "Are you watermelon people?" We replied that we were tourists from New York. So the bus driver announced that we were tourists, and everyone on the bus smiled.

The plane glides low over the Caribbean Sea, and Mango Jack sleeps, droplets of sweat still on his brow. Douglas and Natalie, the people from the dock, who have now become our traveling companions, snuggle in their seats. Melanie studies the guidebook, and I keep watching out the window, looking for the island where we'll rest.

After we land, Jack drops us off at a beach bar in Roatán. He asks us to keep an eye on his suitcase and tells us to wait while he looks for Charlie. The beach resort he wants to take us to is accessible only by speedboat, and Charlie has the only speedboat he'll sit down in.

Douglas tries to pick up the suitcase and says it feels as if Jack is carrying a ton of bricks. Natalie, his "spiritual companion," orders a fruit salad, which arrives with dead gnats in it. Douglas picks the gnats out while Natalie looks away. "They're God's creatures, too," Douglas says, and Natalie smiles weakly.

The town is covered with mud, and the houses stand on stilts to protect them from hurricanes and rising seas. On the beach three boys are having a knife fight, and we watch them impassively in the heat. Vultures sit in the trees, gazing down like spectators at a sporting event. Melanie asks our companions how long they've been in El Salvador. Douglas says they got "the calling" a few years back. Their mission, he tells us, is to save some small "chunk of the world."

Douglas and Natalie tell us that they've just been legally married by a priest in El Salvador, but they'd been spiritually married long before. They work in agricultural reform and are taking their honeymoon. They take a honeymoon every year to "renew their vows to one another." Natalie has heard that there are redheaded woodpeckers indigenous only to the Bay Islands of the Caribbean, and she's anxious to see the woodpeckers. Douglas says he can already feel the energy of the islands infusing his veins.

"So how long have you guys been together?" Douglas asks. We say we've been on the road for two months and that this is the last leg of our journey. We can tell they think we are a couple, and we do nothing to change their minds.

Mango Jack wanders back. "Can't find Charlie anywhere," he tells us. "Might be on a binge, so I made a reservation for us for the night at a guest house up the road."

We follow him, wading through mud and swatting sand fleas. We approach a battered house with unpainted clapboards and windows with torn screens. It has a wraparound porch on the top floor and on that porch sit four men in open khaki shirts. Drinking beer, they gaze down at us. They purse their lips and seem to nod as we reach the steps. One of them, with a dark mustache, spits on the porch.

The Creole woman who runs the place puts us in three rooms on the top floor. Melanie's and mine is dark and dingy, with no screens on the windows and no lock on the door, which is a screen with a large rip in the side. The room is across from the bathroom and smells of the toilet. The sea smells of dead fish, and no breeze comes in. "This isn't what I had in mind." Melanie sighs. "That guy, Mango Jack, he looks to me like he's had a sex-change operation" are Melanie's last words to me as she heads for the shower, a towel across her arm.

She comes back in a few moments. There is no shower. We have to wash in a sink that's on the porch near where the four men stay. I've known Melanie for seven years; there are two essential things for her sense of well-being. She must be clean and she must have someone to flirt with. Melanie asks me to go with her and I grab my towel.

The men sit on the porch near the sink. They have a large pile of beer bottles, shaped like a fortress. We slowly fill the sink with water and begin to wash our faces. Melanie runs a wet brush through her long blond hair. The men smile and ask in a rough Spanish where we are from. I say New York. One has a brother in New York, and he goes into his room and returns with a T-shirt of the Empire State Building which we admire.

We ask where they're from, and they grin. From far away, they tell us. From another world. A distant planet. Melanie puts her hands on her hips a little coyly. She asks if they are watermelon people, and the man who spit before shakes his head and spits again.

Mango Jack still doesn't have money, but he says as soon as we get to the beach resort he'll cash a check with the owner and pay us back. He says he tried to get cash in town, but he'd been foolish enough to forget his checkbook. He knows a nice "restaurant" up the beach, so we follow him there. The restaurant is a thatched hut on the beach that serves rice and beans and the catch of the day. Jack seems to know everybody in town. He orders for us, telling the waiter in his Spanish, spoken with a Texas accent, to bring us shrimp in their special garlic sauce and to fry some plantains.

He seems to know so much that Melanie decides to ask him what watermelon people are. "What are *gente de la sandía?*" she says. He smiles and pushes back slightly from the table. He explains that it is a joke on the Sandinistas. *Sandía* sounds like Sandino. He says some people in this part of the world think the Sandinistas are puffed up but empty inside. Douglas asks Mango Jack what he thinks, and he replies, "Me, I've got no opinion. Except they're all rotten down here."

"Can you imagine?" Melanie says to me with a laugh. "A bus driver thought we were Sandinistas."

"I think he was just teasing you," Mango Jack says, looking us over with a playful grin. "Believe me," he goes on, "I know the ropes in this neck of the woods. There's not a gringo who's been through Central America like I have." He tells us he prefers the coast of Honduras. It's more peaceful. Costa Rica's nice but dull. He spent time in Panajachel till things got bad there. He goes, he tells us, wherever trouble isn't. "So," he says, "if I'm here now, consider yourselves safe."

Douglas says that he's always been safe. He believes some special energy exists in the universe and that if you tap it, you'll be safe. Life, he says, will protect you if you respect it. Melanie, who grew up in California, immediately recognizes this as hot-tub mentality and rolls her eyes. Natalie tells proudly that she signs all her letters "Soul" or "Flight." She says she and Douglas have had a religious experience that changed their lives.

Melanie tries to be polite. "How was it religious?"

"It happened on Christmas," Natalie replies.

But Douglas is quick to interrupt. "Christmas was just a coincidence." They'd been camping in the rain forest of

Hawaii and he'd gotten pneumonia. "I was going to die," he says, "right there in the middle of that rain forest."

"So we prayed." Natalie's voice trembles. "We held hands all night and said a mantra over and over."

"In the morning I was cured," Douglas announces with great feeling.

"And it was Christmas," Natalie says.

"I believe in faith." Mango Jack suddenly speaks. "Some very bad things have happened to me, but I've never lost my faith."

Douglas nods. "I feel what you're saying, man."

"I know I look strange," Mango Jack goes on. "People don't know what to make of me. Do you know I've been refused hotel rooms? Once a guy punched me out in Atlanta, just for walking down the street."

Douglas shakes his head sadly back and forth.

"I've got no home," Jack says. He points somewhere north. "America's a sick place, don't you agree? Don't you guys just hate America?"

Douglas says everywhere is home if you are at peace. Natalie says she doesn't hate anything, not even mosquitoes. Douglas comments on how Natalie won't even swat a mosquito that's sucking blood from her arm. Melanie and I pay for Mango Jack's dinner. Then we wander back to the guest house to sleep.

In the middle of the night one of the men from the porch comes into our room. He has put his hand through our screen and opened the door. Melanie turns on the light and shouts at him, "What are you doing?"

"Excuse me." He looks bewildered. "I am lost." He staggers out and we hear him collapse in front of the bathroom door.

Melanie crawls into bed with me. We are naked in the tropical heat and I feel her skin against my skin. Her breath in my ear. Our breasts touch. I feel her nipples against my flesh, and she trembles. "I'm afraid of myself in this place," she tells me.

In the morning we wake to the sound of gunfire nearby. Actually, it is more like shelling. A low whistling sound followed by a big boom. It is rhythmic and consistent, one shell after another. Melanie looks at me and we jump out of bed, hitting the floor. We huddle next to each other as the shelling goes on. But then it seems to go on too long. After a while we grow bored and slip into our clothes. Carefully we make our way to the porch.

Three of the men are on the porch, beer bottles surrounding them, some rolling around the porch. The fourth still lies dead drunk beside the toilet, where we heard him collapse during the night. Natalie and Douglas peer from their screen door, a sheet pressed against them. "What's going on?" Douglas asks, looking very pale.

We hear the sound of shelling again. One of the men holds up a cage, laughing. Inside is a small green parrot. They tell us her name is Juanita and she is their mascot. They tell us she has survived many shellings in Managua and she is a member of the National Guard. She has learned the language of shellings and she is a survivor. She is a Somocista. They hold up Juanita's cage proudly. The parrot makes the sound of shelling again. Then bursts out laughing.

After a breakfast of bitter coffee and a stale roll, Mango Jack runs off to try to find Charlie again and get us to the beach resort. "I'm working out a contingency plan," Jack tells us, "just in case Charlie is on a real binge. Trust me," he says, and he's gone.

We pay for his breakfast and go back to the guest house. Natalie and Douglas are beginning to get nervous about the possibility of having to stay in this town much longer, and Natalie longs to find the redheaded woodpeckers, so they leave us in search of the ethereal spirit of the island in the hope that it will enter their bodies and enliven them.

Melanie and I sit on our porch, trying to work out our own contingency plan. "We could fly right to Miami," she suggests. I am not opposed to the possibility, though our ticket is back from Panama City. A radio plays more Bee Gees, and an old woman with no teeth comes to sell us warm Pepsis.

The Nicaraguans stagger out of their room and plunk themselves beside us. Their drunk friend has waked, and he sits near me. I give him my Pepsi because he looks thirsty. "You trying to get to the Bay side," one of them says, and we nod. "That crazy guy with you, he won't get you nowhere."

Melanie says she was beginning to figure that out for herself. "We got boat," one of them says. "We got good boat."

We nod. I wish they would leave us alone, but Melanie seems to be enjoying the attention. "Oh, yeah," she says. "Where's your boat?"

"Boat's right down there." One of them points to the reeds behind the guest house. "You wanta see?"

Out of boredom, Melanie cocks her head, shakes out her blond hair, and stands up. "Sure," she says. "Let's see their boat." I make a face at her, but she's heading to the steps. I say to her in English that I'm not sure it's a good idea. But the drunk one has passed out again. There are three of them, two of us. The odds feel all right. We walk down to the water. The one in the Empire State Building T-shirt says, "You sure you not watermelon people?" We say we are Manhattan people, and he laughs.

Among the reeds we spot a small boat with a folded sail. It is fairly well hidden; we have to go through palm fronds to get to it. One of them points. "Good boat. Got us here all right." He lifts the sail and underneath we see an arsenal of rifles, machine guns, and ammunition. Melanie puts her hand across her mouth as she gasps. We both start to walk backward.

But two of them stand behind us now and the other reaches down and pulls out a gun. He lifts the rifle into the air and laughs. He hands the gun to me. "Good U.S. rifle. We got good contact. He sell us rifles. Feel this gun." I've never held a gun before and I'm not sure I want to now, but two of them are standing behind us. I reach out for the rifle. "It has a nice balance," I say, thinking that this sounds like a good thing to say about a gun. I feel Melanie's arm trembling against me.

They all lean toward us. "We take you to the Bay side," the one with the mustache who spits on the ground says. "We got time. We got nothing but time." The one in the T-shirt strokes Melanie's hair. Then he touches her breasts with cupped hands. I feel a hand reach between my thighs and I shove the gun back into the belly of the one with the T-shirt. I clutch Melanie by the hand and we run.

"We got nothing but time," they shout as we scramble up the beach, through the reeds, as fast as we can back to the guest house. We hear them laughing, and one of them imitates the sound of shelling that Juanita made.

Mango Jack comes to tell us he's made a little progress with the speedboat. He tells us to check out of the hotel and he'll be back for lunch. We pay the bill and head to the beach restaurant to wait for him. As we sit there, Melanie, who has been pale all morning, points in the direction of the reeds. "Look," she says. I follow her hand and see Mango Jack, tiny and dark, dragging his huge suitcase down toward the water with the Nicaraguans.

We wait the rest of the day, sipping warm Cokes, but he never returns. It takes a while for it to sink in. He left us just as easily as he found us, and we are now short a

fair amount of cash. Natalie and Douglas join us at the
beach restaurant, and when we tell them we've been swin-
dled, Douglas makes some inane comment about how it
will all come back to us in time.

Melanie is not interested in his theory of eternal return.
She's interested only in getting to Miami. She says to me,
"We could just go to the airport and wait." That is when
the boat arrives. A black man with a nice smile comes up
and introduces himself as Andrew, Charlie's brother-in-law.
"Charlie, he not going anywhere for a long time." His
brother-in-law laughs.

"Where's Mango Jack?" Melanie inquires foolishly, and
Andrew laughs again. "Did he tell you to come get us?"

"That he did, the little gun-runner," he says. "The little
gun-runner, he gone."

Andrew's boat is a small speedboat that takes us around
to Shark's Bay, where the rich people live. It is only a thirty-
minute ride. In the boat Andrew tries to sell us shells. He
has conchs and mother-of-pearl and small colored-shell
necklaces. Melanie, trying to be nice, buys one. Then he
tries to sell us a shark's jaw. He holds up the huge jaw.
"A hammerhead," Andrew tells us. "He got seven rows of
teeth and the teeth all open when the animal ready to
strike." Andrew runs his fingers over the teeth.

We don't feel very comfortable in the boat. "Let me tell
you," Andrew says, "every fish out there that you eat, she
eat you. The worst is a snapper. Snapper can go to a thousand pounds. Or cuda. One bite from a cuda and you never
walk again.

"They all out there. You eat 'em for dinner. They have
you for lunch." He lifts his arm high over the sea. "These
waters don't look dangerous. Look nice and gentle and blue.
But you've been traveling in a wild, crazy sea."

Melanie won't go in the water when we get to the beach
resort. For two days she just sits. "But you love the water,"

I tell her, and she shakes her head. She sits and stares at the sea as if she'll never look at it in the same way again. I swim alone and am chased by a barracuda. It follows my gold bracelet and I see its teeth at my heels. Finally I agree to fly back to Miami.

As we are about to leave, we pause for a while on the porch of our hotel with Douglas and Natalie. A redheaded woodpecker, the first Natalie has seen, lands in a nearby tree and she gets all excited. "Oh, Dougy, look, a wood-pecker."

Douglas says, "See, I told you. You've just gotta be-lieve."

I hoist on my pack. "Douglas, are you going back across the Honduran border?"

He looks at me as if I am a lost soul. If the spirit enters your body, he tells us, you are invincible. You are safe. He points to the sky as the woodpecker, indigenous only to these islands, startled, flies away.

The Hall of the Meteorites

BEFORE I LIKED MEN, I liked rocks. I liked to wander the bluffs and ravines where I grew up and collect smooth, weathered stones. I put them on my shelves where other girls kept dolls and stuffed animals, and with my books on geology I identified and labeled them. Slate, mica, quartz, limestone, granite. What I found in the outside world, I brought into the house. Baby birds who'd fallen from nests, spiders that spun endless webs inside jars with punctured lids, the luna moth I captured as a caterpillar and released one spring day when it emerged from the cocoon it had woven in my room.

My mother taught me what I know of dinosaurs. She'd studied biology and wanted to be a teacher of life sciences. Instead, she had three children. But she kept a great love for the giant reptiles that had roamed the earth, for the minerals and elements, for outer space. In the cold wintery Saturdays of my youth, she would take me in the car downtown and we'd visit the Field Museum.

We always began in the Hall of the Dinosaurs, where she'd try to explain how these animals had lived before any of us were born. Often she'd joke and say even before *she* was born, but it was beyond me that anything had lived before, or would live after, me. I was fascinated by the bones of these long-dead creatures, and there was a place where children could reach up and rub a dinosaur's knee, smooth and hard as stones.

The one that amazed me the most was the giant marine lizard. There was a picture of it swimming in an incredibly rough sea and a sign that told how its remains had been found in a chalk bed in Kansas. I'd been to Kansas to visit an aunt, and there was no sea in Kansas. When I asked my mother about this, she just said that things change.

We would end our day at the planetarium sky show, where the lights dimmed and the heavens were illuminated overhead. A great disembodied voice would tell us, as we twisted our necks back and craned upward to see, that the universe was infinite, and if you traveled across it in a straight line, you'd end up right back where you started.

Much of this was lost on me, and I would grow tired, trying to understand, but my mother always wanted to stay for hours. Sometimes she'd try to stall before going home. She'd ask me if I wanted to look at the Hall of the Mammals again, if I wanted to buy some new stones for my collection. But usually I just wanted to go home. She'd look sad as we passed the glass cases filled with minerals and gems, the bones of great reptiles, on our way home.

Once as we walked to the car, the harsh wind blowing off Lake Michigan, my mother told me there was a whole side of life I hadn't seen yet and that none of it would make sense to me until I was as old as she, as old as a time that seemed as distant to me as the age of reptiles, as far away as the visions of the planetarium sky.

In eighth grade I discovered boys. I discovered them the same way I'd discovered rocks and butterflies and dinosaur bones. My mother explained them to me. She handed me a pink book one day and said, "Study this the way you study anything else. Then you'll know." And she added, "Well, you'll almost know."

I had known before that boys existed. I'd seen them putting on their baseball uniforms for Little League and I'd had snowball fights with them after school. But I'm not sure I understood what they were doing there. I'd always viewed them not as another sex, but as another species, as if I attended classes and went roller-skating with giraffes. But then one day my mother told me all, and I simply assumed I could apply my cataloguing spirit to them as well.

I thought I could collect and label whatever came my way, but I found myself at parties in darkened rooms with unknown entities, unidentifiable objects. Dancing in the dark, I touched bones, the muscles, the veins that coursed through their arms. I detected their scent, which at the time was mostly a cologne called Canoe, mingled with the pungent smell of athletic sweat.

I also began discovering things about my family. My father, for instance, developed a passion for woodworking. He devoted every spare moment to making chairs, tables, hatracks. He paneled the basement and turned it into a recreation room. He paneled bathrooms and put wooden frames around the bathtubs. All night and all day on weekends, after work, we heard him sawing, hammering, sanding.

During dinner, his fingers thumped on the tablecloth, eager to begin his hammering again. My mother said to him that we had enough chairs, enough tables. But he couldn't stop. He said he was doing it for us. Making the house beautiful for us. He constructed a new fence around the yard to protect us. His hammering became a clock, ticking away in my life, and when he'd built everything he could think to build, he was gone.

I went east to college and fell in love there for the first time. I fell in love with my lab partner, Benjamin Eiseman. I was pre-med, and we shared a lab bench, where we spent the weeks of Indian summer dissecting dogfish, frogs, cats. We opened a cat together, delicately prying it apart, and named every muscle, every vein. Benjamin was huge and clumsy, and at times our hands grazed as we worked inside animals. Before I knew what was happening, I fell in love with him.

One night he called to ask if I wanted to see a film. He said that *Superfluid* was playing at the physics department. We sat watching a film about the properties of a special liquid and all the time I was aware of the way his arm felt as it rested against mine. After the film, we drank Cokes in a café, then walked out onto the library roof. It was 1965, and as we stood on the roof, the lights of the entire city were suddenly obliterated. The night was as dark as a country road and we stood there for hours, holding hands. Then, when the lights began to come on, he turned me to him and kissed me. We stayed on the roof of that library, kissing until all the lights of the northeast came back on again.

We began an experiment. We carved windows into the shells of fertilized chicken eggs and covered the windows with isinglass. Under the light of the incubator in the lab we watched chickens grow — the formation of wings, of tiny beaks. And I saw the single path upon which my life was heading. I would marry Benjamin after college and we would have children. He would go to medical school and I would become a teacher of life sciences.

Then one night, after we'd been seeing one another for six weeks, he picked me up at my dorm and told me about Sarah. It was winter and he walked me over to the track, then began walking around the track, circling and circling, little clouds of breath rising from his lips. "I've got to tell you something," he said, "I should have told you a long time ago." We continued walking. "I never should have let it get this far." What he meant by that was that one night he had told me he loved me and we'd made love, my first time, in his dorm room while his roommate was out of town.

I can find no label for what I felt that night. Though it was almost twenty years ago and at an early stage in my history, the image is perfectly clear. We walked in that circle around the track, we walked for miles I think, and he told that he was in love with a girl he'd known since he was fourteen. That she sent him brownies that were still hot, that she knitted him the sweater he was wearing so that he'd be warm. That he planned to marry her as soon as college was done.

The earth, my mother had taught me, seeks equilibrium. Volcanoes erupt, hurricanes blow, forests ignite, all so that the earth can re-establish its balance. Nature, she'd told me, has its secret plan. I tried to devise my own and failed. I became obsessed with Benjamin.

He asked if I would keep seeing him and give him some time to make up his mind. I gave him four years. I could not get him out of my mind for a moment. I was like the robin who hears the worm in the ground. My head was cocked. I sensed his presence. I heard his footsteps when he walked into the lab. I knew when Sarah would be coming down, and once, when I saw them together, I followed them at a distance. I followed them for a long time as they walked around campus and I studied them. I noticed how their feet were not in sync, how her body met his well below the shoulder so that he looked as if he were straining when he walked with his arm around her.

I waited him out. I played hard to get, then gave him ultimatums. I would refuse to see him; then I would give in. For four years he begged me to be patient with him. He would see me during the week and then see Sarah on the weekend. He told me each week that he was going to make a decision soon. One week he did. He married Sarah right after graduation. He wrote once to say they were happy and were about to have a child. When the child was born, they sent me an announcement. It had a little bird on it, sitting in a nest. I never wrote him back.

It took me years to get back on the track. I moved to another city. I dated other men, but none struck me the way Benjamin had. It was around this time that my parents separated. I'd known it was coming, but that didn't make it any easier. She called me shortly after I got the baby announcement from Benjamin and sobbed that her life was over, that she didn't know what to do. I flew to the midwest and helped her settle into an apartment. Then I got on with my own life.

I relinquished my interest in natural history and became an identifier and cataloguer of primitive art. At times I traveled to faraway places and examined important discoveries to determine their worth, to situate them in time. I was very good at cooking utensils, weapons, and sacred idols. It was on such an expedition that I accidently met the man who was to become my husband.

I was on a flight to Brazil, and a man sat next to me. He was a large, middle-aged man, and his feet had trouble fitting into the seat. He kept crossing and uncrossing his knees and finally said to me, "I travel so much, you'd think I'd remember to get an aisle." His name was Martin Garnet. He was a doctor who traveled to isolated places to set up medical clinics. He wore Old Spice, and I was quick to pick up the scent.

He called me when we both got back to the States and we began seeing each other. He was just getting over a bad marriage. I was still getting over Benjamin, though I'd begun to be interested in men again. We both traveled a lot, and when we could, we saw one another. He brought me gifts from duty-free shops all over the world, which I placed on a special shelf. Carved fish, shark's-teeth necklaces, miniature paintings on wood. He came back with fabulous stories about childbirth made painless by acupuncture, surgery done by hand, chronic illness cured by visits to the local oracle. I listened for hours to his tales of India, the jungles of Peru, and slowly, though I hadn't intended to, I began to care for him.

Martin defied classification. When I told him I'd never met anyone like him before, he replied, "There is no one like me." And he was correct. In the early stage of our courtship I should have had a sense of what life with Martin would be like. Once he was on a trip to the West Coast and had a day stopover before flying to Europe. He called to say he didn't think he could see me between trips because he needed to go to Brooklyn to get a pair of dress pants. "Pants?" I said over the phone. "Don't they have pants in Portland?" But he said he was on a tight schedule and didn't think he had time to buy pants. I told him to get his pants and keep walking in them.

But he didn't. He stayed. Then he went. He traveled to Pakistan, then came back for two days before leaving for L.A. Whenever he came back, he told me wonderful stories about what he'd seen and done. Then he'd leave again. I found myself traveling less, wanting to be with him more, and I found Martin, once he felt secure with me, traveling all the time. While he was in Brazil, I wrote him a letter. I said I was a fighting fish on a strong line and I was trying to get away. I didn't mail the letter. Instead, I tucked it into my appointment calendar.

One night Martin and I quarreled, because as soon as he got back from Brazil he had to leave for Nigeria. I left his place in a huff, got into a cab, and forgot my appointment calendar in the taxi. When I got home, I turned off my phone and took a long, hot bath. When I emerged, the light to my answering machine blinked. I knew it was Martin, calling to patch things up, saying he wasn't going to Nigeria after all.

Instead, the message said, "Hello, Monica Alberts. For

a successful curator, you should put your name in your appointment calendar. I now know that your mother's name is Rochelle, that your parents have separated and your mother lives in Madison, that you are supposed to go to Peru in June, and that you had drinks with Betsy this afternoon. I'm afraid I woke Betsy up when I called, so you should apologize for me. Forgive me, but I also read your letter to Martin in an attempt to track you down. It's obvious that guy is driving you crazy, and my advice is don't marry him. I don't mean to pry, but that's my opinion. My name is Arnold Schnackler and I work in a lunar-receiving laboratory." He gave me the name of his university and phone numbers where he could be reached.

Arnold Schnackler's office wall was decorated with a map of the universe. His bedroom ceiling was filled with Day-Glo stars, and he'd teach me the names of the various constellations before we fell asleep. His work was studying objects coming from the moon that struck the earth, and he was devoted to finding life in outer space. He was also devoted to finding life on earth, and for a few weeks we had a good time.

Then Martin called from Nigeria one night when I wasn't home and left a grief-stricken message. He cut his trip short and came home. Arnold told me I was making the mistake of my life, but I said, "What can you do when love hits you over the head." When Martin came home, he said he wasn't going to travel much anymore. He wanted to be with me. And one night he proved it by handing me, over dinner, a large diamond. "Here," he said. "Add this to your collection of rocks."

Martin's heart was in the right place. But it wasn't with me. I thought, from what he'd promised, that love would make him want to travel less. Instead, it seemed to make him want to travel more. He traveled all over the world, dropping off his laundry between flights, and delivered papers on how to set up rural hospitals. He received super bonuses from all the airlines' advantage travel programs, and when he got these bonuses, he took me along if I could go.

When I told him I wanted a child, he agreed and traveled more. I thought of my father, building endless chairs and tables we didn't need, and how my mother was more alone with him than without him, how she begged him to stop. I understood now that some men couldn't stop.

Sometimes when Martin was away, I'd stand on the balcony of our building in Brooklyn and look at the stars. I wondered which ones were shining over him and what presents he'd bring me when he returned. But then I would feel lonely; once I tried to call Arnold Schnackler, the man from the lunar-receiving laboratory, to ask him if he'd discovered life in outer space and to tell him I could still name the constellations.

I found something happening to me. I found myself becoming a little cold inside, a little hard. It was as if a lump were in the middle of my chest, some solid thing I couldn't name. I called my mother once when I felt this way. I said to her, "I don't know myself anymore." And there was nothing she could say.

When Martin was back from one of his trips but about to leave again, I planned a romantic evening. I served dinner by candlelight and we drank champagne. Then I said, "How about if we go upstairs and get in bed?" and Martin said that was fine, but he was expecting two international calls, and if I didn't mind, he'd like to take them when they come in.

I stood up to clear the table and began rinsing and stacking the dishes. Martin said, "Darling, you shopped and cooked. I'll do the dishes."

I raised my fist high above the sink and brought it down flat on the dishes, smashing them to bits. "Then do them," I said, and I walked away.

We went to a marriage counselor to get back on a good track. The counselor suggested, since it was difficult for us to find time together, that we plan nice things to do that would be special, and that way we would have things to look forward to. She said that I needed to be more relaxed about time and Martin needed to be more attentive. It seemed simple enough. So when we stopped seeing the marriage counselor, Martin said, "Your birthday is coming up in three months. Let's plan something nice." I suggested a picnic in the country, a climb on Bear Mountain. A quiet evening at home.

Six weeks before my birthday Martin told me he was excited because he'd been invited to the Soviet Union for a four-day conference on international health. I was very excited for him. Then he told me the dates and I reminded him that he was going to the Soviet Union over my birthday. He promised he'd be back in time to celebrate.

A few days before my birthday and his departure for the Soviet Union we went to dinner in a Chinese restaurant and I said, "Let's plan my birthday now." And he said he'd be back at seven in the morning and would come right home for a champagne toast. Then he said he just had two little things he had to do that day. He had to have breakfast with a health counselor from Martinique at eight-thirty and then lunch with some people from Saudi Arabia. "But the rest of the day I'm yours."

I spent my birthday alone, climbing Bear Mountain, and when I got off the mountain, I decided to give him one more chance. When I met him in the evening, I said, "I've never been bored with you, but I've never been so alone." Martin understood. He wanted to make it up to me. We

planned our anniversary. We decided we'd spend a weekend in Vermont. It was September when Martin told me he had been invited to Afghanistan and I reminded him that he was going to Afghanistan over our anniversary. He said, "Maybe they can get somebody else."
And I said, "Maybe I can."

When I decided to move out, I called my mother to ask if she'd help me, and my father answered the phone. I said, "What're you doing there, Dad?" and he hesitated, then cleared his throat. He said he was living with my mother again. I said, "That's not possible."
And he replied, "Anything can happen in this world."
My mother came to help me move, the way I had helped her. She organized my closets and helped me pick out sheets and towels. She seemed to me vague and distant, and when I asked about my father, she told me, "It was easier this way." When she kissed me good-bye, she imparted her final wisdom. "There are some things," she said, "you have to find out for yourself."
I dug my way into a deep hole, from which I did not emerge for months. I went into a cave in which I found myself regressing in time, growing wild, primitive. I subscribed to *Natural History* and learned things I'd never known. Trees grow only if there is space between them, but if there are no other trees around, they'll burn out in the sun. Baby monkeys will choose a mother that cuddles over one that feeds. And sharks are missing the enzyme that produces anxiety. They go through the deep without depression or fear. I wanted to become a shark.

In the spring I emerged and released myself back into the world. I was learning the fine art of being alone, and I had almost mastered it when, while walking through the park one day, I heard someone calling my name. I turned to see a stranger, jumping up and down, shouting "Monica, is that you?" I saw a middle-aged man, rather stout and gray, his hairline receding. Yet he knew me, so I approached tentatively. "Benjamin," he said. "Benjamin Eiseman. You remember, the blackout, 1965."

I was shocked to think I had not recognized him. We hugged, and his arms felt flaccid; I was aware of his belly against mine.

Over coffee he told me that Sarah kicked him out about two years ago. "She hooked up with some guy who sells software in a computer store." Benjamin shook his head in disbelief. He told me that he'd never finished medical school because their baby died of heart failure, and that he taught biology in a high school in the town where he grew up. "Not what we expected, is it?"

I told him about the demise of my marriage and agreed with him. "Nobody told us it would be like this." I found I had little to say to him. As we paid the bill, he said, "So, do you still think about me?"

To my surprise, I realized that I hadn't thought of him in years. I hadn't thought of him at all since I'd been with Martin. "I've become obsessed with other things," I said.

I headed home, stunned by my encounter with Benjamin, thrown off course again, and wondering if I should move ahead with my divorce or try to work things out with Martin, as he wanted. I knew the answer would never again be a simple yes or no. Rather, it would be a slow unwinding, like a battery running down, decision by attrition.

I passed the Museum of Natural History. I didn't want to go back to my apartment right away, so I wandered in. I moved aimlessly through the museum, like a person trying to find something she's lost but can't quite remember what it is. I went into the Hall of the Dinosaurs, but they didn't seem so big anymore and I felt uneasy with their bones. I wandered downstairs. Through the Hall of Mammals,

Primitive Man, Arctic Animals. I visited the ancestors' exhibit, but it didn't move me, either.

Then I saw the sign for the Hall of the Meteorites, and I went in. I watched a brief film that told how meteorites are the Rosetta stones of outer space, how they enable us to grasp the wonder of the world. I saw pictures of the wilderness of Siberia, where in Tunguska a giant fireball struck the earth and caused brushfires to burn for two decades. I walked around the small meteorites that lined the room, and they all had names: Gibeon, Guffy, Knowles, Diable.

And then in the middle of the room I paused in front of the greatest meteorite of them all, Ahnighito, which struck Greenland ten thousand years earlier and which the Eskimos believed had been hurled to the earth by the gods. Weighing thirty-one tons, Ahnighito is solid iron and parts have been polished where you can touch it.

Above the meteorites is a mirror, and I saw where coins had been tossed for good luck. Ahnighito means the Tent, and there are two other meteorites that were once part of Ahnighito. They are the Woman and the Dog. The tent, the woman, the dog — the simple needs of domesticity, all that is required for the happy life.

I reached up to rub the shiny part of the meteorites and thought of my hand, when I was a child, rubbing the knees of dinosaurs. I thought of my mother, giving my father another chance in the midwest; I tossed a penny on top of the Tent and saw in the mirror where it landed. Suddenly I realized that I was the same age as my mother when she first had brought me to the museum and taught me what she could of the world.

When I left, the sky had turned gray. I looked up and knew I'd never look at it in the same way again. That now I knew anything can strike us at any time. I contemplated the simple things and felt as I walked how easy it is for a heart to turn to stone.

Losing Your Cool

SALLY MITCHELL believed in fate. She had been literally looking the other way when she met Pete, so she believed it was meant to be. Now she believed she was being tested. Lately things hadn't been going Sally's way. They hadn't exactly been going against it, either. There were simply "complications," as Pete told her the other night when he suggested they forget about their plan of living together for the summer.

Sally had spent summers in the city ever since her father had driven her across the Queensboro Bridge three years ago, helped her move into the small L-shaped studio, and said, "Well, kid, you're on your own now." She'd worked as a waitress for a while and served coffee on roller skates. She'd learned word processing and did weekend jobs for large law firms. She'd wanted to be an actress on a soap opera, but so far nothing had happened.

She had been looking forward to spending the summer with Pete in Jersey, but a few nights before he'd come over and said he thought they should wait on their summer plans. She was used to him changing their plans. She'd grown to anticipate it. Pete shared custody of Jaspar, his

six-year-old son, and now his wife wanted him to take
Jaspar for all of July and August, and he said he thought
it would be best if they just saw each other on weekends.

Pete lived in Jersey and drove a Coca-Cola truck. In the
evenings he went to school to learn to be a CPA. When
Pete didn't have school and didn't have Jaspar with him,
he saw Sally. Sally had thought that by this summer Jaspar would want to meet her, but he still said no. So Sally
was stuck in the city.

Sally was upset when she called her father, but he just
said, "Count your blessings." She counted them. She had
a little apartment that looked out on an airshaft, but she'd
made it as nice as she could. She had a boyfriend who
picked her up in a red and white striped Coca-Cola shirt
that made people stop in restaurants and say, "Where can
I get a shirt like that?" And Pete would reply, "Join the
Teamsters." She had a small plastic card that gave her
money from the bank when she had it, and she had a cat
she'd found in a tree, named Katmandu.

What she didn't have was an air conditioner. Actually,
she had one but it had blown out a while ago. It belonged
to her crazy landlord, Antonio Petrocelli, and he'd offered
it as a luxury he was including with the apartment. The
first summer it was all right, but then she had to start the
fan by giving it a turn with her hand. She'd open the thing
up and take out the filter and give the fan a twirl and
eventually it would pick up speed. But it got slower and
slower, making a noise like a meat grinder, and one day it
died.

It had died at the end of summer last year, and Sally
planned to replace it. But then one night in Jersey Pete had
said, when things were going well, "Hey, why don't you
sublet that place of yours and come live with me next
summer?" Sally had gotten out of bed and looked out the
window. Outside stood the Coca-Cola truck, parked in the

driveway, all red and white, looking cool and serene, with
its empties stacked in neat cases inside. Sally had taken a
deep breath, like a diver preparing for the plunge.

Pete came over with a case of Cokes wrapped in a red ribbon. "Just thought I'd make it up to you for the change in
summer plans. This should carry you through." He popped
one open with his teeth. Pete had a million ways of opening a bottle of Coke. He could do it with a dime; he could
twist it on the edge of almost any piece of furniture. He
could even crack the lip of the glass so that no glass would
go in. He sat down at the kitchen table, across the room
from her, and fanned himself with an old magazine.

"I'm upset," Sally said.

"Look, honey" — Pete leaned back in the chair — "I
know I've disappointed you, but Jaspar's still not ready to
have a new mother. We've got to think about the future."

Sally had heard this many times in the past year. Jaspar
had agreed to tell his father when he was ready to meet
Sally, and so far Jaspar wasn't ready. Sally pulled her chair
near him and drank from his Coke. "Oh, I understand your
predicament." She tried to decide if she really did understand, but then pushed that thought away. "But I just dread
having to deal with Mr. Petrocelli."

She pointed to the old air conditioner. Mr. Petrocelli had
given Sally a hard time before. He'd tried to evict her when
Katmandu had gotten on the roof. He came screaming into
her apartment once when her neighbor's stereo was on,
thinking it was hers. She didn't think she could deal with
Mr. Petrocelli. But she was pretty sure she could deal with
Pete.

Sally had met Pete on a sweltering day at Jones Beach.
He'd just separated from his wife and was having one of
his first outings with a group of friends. They'd brought a
huge cooler of Cokes and beers. While Sally and her friend

Tracy, who taught exercise classes at the TrimTime Health
Club, put their toes in the oily water, she had noticed Pete
looking at her, and she'd looked at him.

Sally had often wondered how things happen between
people. Pete sat on his towel, drinking a beer, and the next
thing she knew he was standing next to her. He said, "I
like the Jersey shore better, but my friends wanted to come
here." Some spark had flown. Something inexplicable and
strange. A few nights later in bed he told her that she really
turned him on. Their lovemaking had been a slow build,
and since that night she'd always missed his body when it
wasn't next to hers.

Because of the unexpected heat wave in June, it would take
a week for the new air conditioner to be installed. In the
morning Sally had taken a deep breath, something she
seemed to be doing often these days, and called Mr. Petrocelli. He'd said to her, "I'ma sicka man. You take out the
air conditioner. You geta new one. Calla my friend Rico
at Cool Cat. He'll take care of you." Sally had called Rico,
and for a price she could afford, he offered to remove the
old a.c. and put in a new one. But it would take a week.

During that week Sally found herself lingering in banks
longer than she needed to. She rode only on air-conditioned buses. She went to movies with Tracy in the middle
of the afternoon and sipped club soda afterward. She and
Pete slept together for a few nights, their bodies keeping a
distance from one another, and finally he said, "Honey,
why don't we just cool it until you get your new unit installed."

On Saturday night Sally went to see her father in Queens.
She sat on one of the twin beds in her father's bedroom
and he sat on the other bed, drinking Heineken's. The
bedroom was the only air-conditioned room in the house,
and the old G.E. hummed as they watched reruns of "Sat-

urday Night Live." One skit was about an actress who only
wanted to make it as a waitress. She'd gone to waitressing
school, studied balancing trays, serving with one hand, but
she was a flop. "All I ever get is leads in Broadway plays,"
she complained.

They'd laughed over the skit. Then Sally reached across
for the phone and tried to call Pete, but there was no answer, so she guessed he was out with Jaspar. It was late
for them to be out, but she decided to wait until the next
skit was over before she tried again. Her father opened
another beer, watching her dial again. He said, "No sense
you keep calling some guy who doesn't come home. You'll
just get yourself all hot and bothered."

"He'll be home later."

Her father moved to an armchair. "So, you decide what
you're going to do with yourself?"

"I'm going to get a new air conditioner."

Her father nodded. "That's as good a place as any to
start." He asked her to turn the cooling up. It was the same
air conditioner that had kept his bedroom cool when her
mother was alive and they'd had the double bed. Sometimes on Sunday afternoons they'd close the door and turn
on the air conditioner, even if it wasn't hot, and stay there
for a while.

Since her mother died, her father's habits had changed.
He had a belly now and he didn't dress as well. He wasn't
so careful about getting the grease out from under his nails
when he came home from his small repair shop. And he
collected things. He rinsed the little cartons from Chinese
food he ate almost every night and stuck things in them.
He labeled the little cartons. Bottle caps, nickels, flat-headed
nails. They lined the shelves. He kept old magazines and
beer cans. Clutter was everywhere. Her mother hated clutter and always threw things away. She'd kept him at bay,
but now he'd returned to what he'd always been. It made

Sally wonder. If she stayed with Pete, what would she keep? What would she give up?

The air conditioning men, Harry and Julio, slipped the old Fedders from the window and put it on the floor. Sweating profusely, they kept asking her for Cokes. "We'll have you cooled off in no time flat."

Julio started sneezing. "You got a cat?"

"In the kitchen," Sally replied.

"I shoulda brought my surgical mask. But we'll be outa here soon."

Harry, who wore a shirt with badges all over it that read KEEP ON TRUCKIN' and DIESEL MAN, seemed to be the boss. He let Julio lug the old a.c. out and bring the new one in while he measured the window. He kept a pencil behind his ear and he tapped the pencil against his ear as he made decisions for the installation of the new machine. "How were you getting that thing started, miss?" Harry said.

"Manual," she replied. "I've been giving it a twist with my hand."

"Coulda lost your hand," Harry said. "This thing's rotten to the core." Julio sneezed several times as he staggered across the room with the new 1984 model Fedders in his arms. Harry slipped in some new panels and set a bar across the window. Sally was amazed at how easy the procedure was. In recent weeks nothing had gone quite this smoothly. She told herself that if she could accomplish this one simple task, she could move on to bigger things. If I can do this, Sally told herself, if I can be a grown-up person and get an air conditioner installed, then I can do anything.

While they were drilling braces for the window, the phone rang. "I just wanted to say hi, honey." Pete was calling from Western Deli, midway through his route. "Scorcher out here."

"Here too, honey. I miss you."

"I miss you too."

There was a pause, so Sally said, "I'm having my new air conditioner installed, so you can come here this weekend if you want."

She heard Pete take a sip of Coke. Then there was silence at the other end. "That's what I'm calling about. Jaspar's been pretty bad this week and Marilyn asked if I couldn't take him to the Watergap this weekend, canoeing." Sally felt the phone, warm in her hand, sweat in her palm.

"Oh," she said. "I guess if he's having a hard time, you should do that."

"I've disappointed you again."

"Well, I know there isn't much you can do about it." Sally sighed. "I tried to call you Saturday night."

The Coke bottle hit the receiver, making a clunking noise. "I didn't get home till real late. Marilyn's been all upset over Jaspar. We had to talk some things out." Sally nodded without speaking. Julio sneezed as he moved the air conditioner across the room. She smiled weakly at the men, then turned her back to them.

"Did you get home at all?" she asked softly.

"Of course I did." His voice was moist on the other end of the phone, and it made her tremble. "You know I did," he whispered, and a wave traveled through her. She thought it was his voice that made her lights go out, surrounding her in darkness. His voice that made the old refrigerator cease its buzzing. That stopped Michael Jackson dead in the middle of a song.

Mr. Petrocelli and his son, Carlo, stood in Sally's living room, screaming. Mr. Petrocelli was a skinny, wiry man with green skin and white saliva that stuck in the corners of his mouth, as if he had rabies. He shouted at her, "You canna put a twelve-amp, twelve-thousand-BTU machine in. The machine I give you it'sa twelve-amps but only ten-thousand BTUs."

Julio and Harry sat on the floor, sipping Cokes, shaking their heads. "The BTUs don't matter," Harry said. "Amps is amps. She took down the whole apartment when she went." Harry tried to explain that he had a little gadget, called a quick starter, that he'd hooked to the back of the machine, and it would pick up extra juice and the machine would be fine if Mr. Petrocelli would just throw on the breaker and let them try it again.

"I'ma not gonna let you try anything again. I gotta key to the basement. It'sa my building and you aren't gonna make me throw on the breaker."

Harry and Julio looked at her. "If he don't throw on the breaker, we can't wait around. You want us to take it out or what?"

"She canna have this machine and I'ma not gonna throw the breaker on."

Sally held up her hands to Mr. Petrocelli. "Now calm down," she said. "Let's be reasonable. Harry, why don't you go get the quick starter while I discuss this further with Mr. Petrocelli."

Harry and Julio left, and the Petrocellis remained. Sally said, "Maybe it's your wiring that's bad. Maybe that's why it happened."

Mr. Petrocelli shouted at her. "I'ma sick man. I canna take this pressure. You call Rico. You tell him to take this out and put a new one in. You geta seven and half amps."

She thought of her Stouffer's spinach soufflé, her Lean Cuisine glazed chicken, her Tropicana orange juice, in the freezer, defrosting. She thought about spending the evening in the dark. She looked at Mr. Petrocelli, his green skin, his white saliva, going on endlessly about amps and BTUs.

Even though she knew better, Sally found herself yelling

at Mr. Petrocelli. She told him she would deal with this herself. She told him she didn't need his help. She told him all he knew how to do was abuse his tenants. She knew she should stop, but she couldn't. Even as she yelled, she thought to herself, I should not be yelling at this crazy man. I should not be having a fight with a lunatic.

The saliva in Mr. Petrocelli's mouth thickened; his face turned a deeper shade of green. Carlo raised his fist to her. "You respect my father. Don't you yell at my father." Mr. Petrocelli had to throw his son against the wall to keep him from hitting her.

Sally sat in the dark and the heat, food spoiling in the icebox, waiting for Harry to return with the new part and speculating on the nature of electricity. She thought that it was something she hadn't understood at all. She didn't know what amps were or BTUs. She hadn't known where her fuse box was until Harry showed her. All her life she'd turned on electrical switches, made toast, dried her hair, typed résumés, without the least understanding of where the power came from. She knew of great generators, of windmills and water-powered turbines. She'd once protested against a nuclear reactor, but how the current made its way from spinning turbines or smashing atoms to her Norelco hair dryer was one of life's great mysteries.

She knew it had to do with positive and negative charges. That some things attracted others to them, others repelled, and this caused friction. Sometimes in the winter when she and Pete kissed on his wall-to-wall carpeting and they were barefoot, they got little shocks on their lips. And sometimes when they got into bed and shook the blanket over them, little blue sparks flew. But where it came from, she never knew.

The air conditioner hummed quietly as Sally listened to a Laura Branigan record and dried her hair. Pete was com-

ing to pick her up in an hour, and she wanted to look nice.
Harry had come back in the early evening and installed the
new piece. It picked up the juice and Harry had had her
put on her stereo. Mr. Petrocelli, under a threat from Sally
to call the police, had thrown the breaker back on. Sally
had climbed into a warm bath after Harry left, feeling exhausted. She wanted to be in good shape when Pete arrived.

When Pete was a half-hour late, Sally began phoning.
When he was an hour late, she found herself getting annoyed. Pete had been arriving later and later. Just a week
ago he'd been half an hour late to meet her bus and had
left her standing there in a heat wave. He'd always been
on time in the past, but now she felt as if small, barely
perceptible things were starting to take place between them.
Sally began to think of all the things he'd been late for. He
hadn't moved ahead with his divorce. And there'd been no
progress in her meeting Jaspar.

Finally there was a knock at her door. She prepared
herself not to be angry as she flung open the door, and she
found Mr. Petrocelli. "Here," he said, "I brought you these.
Delay-Time fuses. A present, from me."

Mr. Petrocelli walked into her apartment. He got on a
kitchen chair and began showing Sally in minute detail how
to test and change her fuses. "You turn it this way, then
you turn it that way." Sally did yoga breathing to keep
herself calm. When he left, he put his green skin, his white
mouth, close to her. "You see" — she felt his hot breath —
"I'ma nicea man."

When Pete arrived two hours later, Sally was furious. All
she said was "You should've called." Over dinner they
quarreled. He had to change their dinner plans for next
Monday night, and Sally felt like a rubber band, pulled
tight, ready to snap. When they got back to the apartment, they weren't speaking much to one another. It was

another hot, muggy night and Sally didn't mind the distance so much. She put on the lights, the stereo. When she put on the air conditioner, the fuses blew.

That night Sally and Pete sat in the dark in her hot apartment, talking about what they were going to do. They discussed the positive and negative aspects of their relationship. Lately they agreed the negative had been more obvious. They had a lot in common; they wanted the same things. But Pete felt Sally put too much pressure on him to be with her, and Sally felt Pete wasn't someone she could count on. Into the night they talked and in the morning they agreed to give it another try. Sally would be more understanding. Pete would be more reliable.

The next morning Harry came over and changed the fuses. As he changed the fuses, the lights came back on. "See," he said, "the quick starter kept it from throwing the breaker." Sally smiled, relieved that she would not have to deal with Mr. Petrocelli. "Now," Harry says, "here's what you gotta do. First put her on fan for about a minute. Then you can switch her to cool, after she's nice and juiced up. Then you put on all your other appliances. Okay?" As he was leaving, he asked her to have dinner with him on Saturday night. Sally stepped back. She said she had a boyfriend, and Harry replied, "Looks like you may have had a boyfriend, but, excuse me, but from the conversation you had on the phone the other day, I'd say he's giving you the boot."

Sally thanked him for changing her fuses and she went to the grocery store, where she lost her temper with the checkout girl, who got mad when she asked for shopping bags after the girl had already begun packing. She got angry with the janitor at the word processing place where she worked because he threw out some papers that were on the floor.

Tuesday, as Sally was waiting for Pete to arrive, he called her. He was whispering into the phone. "I can't talk. I've got an emergency situation here. Marilyn's having a crisis. I can't make it tonight."

Suddenly she found herself shouting at Pete, "What do you mean, you can't make it tonight?"

"I just can't," he whispered.

"If you don't make it," Sally screamed into the phone, "you can forget it!"

"Don't call me. You'll only make it worse."

And he hung up. Sally clutched the phone in her hand, then slammed the receiver down. She did not know what to do with herself. She did not know what to do with her hands. She turned on her stereo. She turned on her lights. She plugged in an iron to iron a shirt. She turned on her air conditioner. She forgot to start at fan, the way Harry had told her to. Instead, she went right to cool and all the fuses blew.

Sally found her flashlight and went to the fuse box. She'd blown a twenty amp and two fifteens. She turned off all her appliances. She did not think she could stand for one more moment to be in the dark. Sally got the fuses out of the drawer and slowly began to change them. The fuses were hot to the touch, and she twisted them out with a rag. When the new fuses were in, she tested to make sure she hadn't thrown the breaker. When she was sure she hadn't, she called her father. "Dad," she said, "my new Fedders keeps blowing my fuses."

"So get another one."

"That simple?" Sally asked.

"You bet," her father said.

In the morning Sally called Cool Cat and said quite calmly into the phone, "Get me another air conditioner." She spoke slowly and with authority. "Get me something that works and doesn't blow my fuses."

While Harry and Julio struggled to remove the new a.c. and install a slightly more expensive Friedrich, which used only seven and a half amps, Sally went out and got them beers. Pete had not called back, and she was wondering when he would. She had hardly slept the night before, waiting to hear from him. At three in the morning she'd called, but there was no answer. She'd poured herself a shot of vodka, something she'd never done before, and went back to sleep.

On her way down Broadway, Jews for Jesus handed her a leaflet. God is a huge electric generator, it said. Jesus is the spark that lights our lives. Faith is the switch we need to turn on.

At seven o'clock the wind picked up. The sky turned black, as if some judgment were upon them. It rained as it hadn't in weeks. Pete called during the storm and told her he'd had to spend the night on Marilyn's sofa. She believed him. She had no reason to doubt him. She was not even angry with him. But she felt some small part of herself turn off, step away. She moved ever so slightly back and found that some of what had been there was gone.

After the rains, the weather broke and the air was cool and crisp. She opened the windows and a breeze blew in. Sally got into bed. The sheets were white and smooth. She curled herself into a small circle and counted herself among the first of her blessings.

Alewives

WHENEVER BUCKY BILL WILSON came to town, he knocked the girls dead. He always came at the same time of year, and every year he picked a new girl for himself for the season. He came for the summers and for a month over Christmas, and when he came to town the boys would tremble.

One year he picked Cindy Michaels. She'd been Gary Thompson's girl for the past few years and they'd gone to all the hops together. Then Bucky picked Cindy, and though she'd tried to fight it, Bucky wasn't someone you'd fight off easily.

During cheerleader practice, Bucky would come to the field and watch Cindy turn and spin and jump in the air. The cheer squad didn't usually practice in the summer, but we really wanted to be ready for the fall; we were certain the Little Giants were going to win state. And most of us had stayed home to go to summer school, anyway. Miss Guerney, who ran the summer school, had agreed to let us use the locker room and playing fields. Every day, after our biology or typing classes, we practiced. We wanted to be able to jump so that our heels touched the back of our heads. Or so that our legs opened in perfect splits.

Bucky was always there, urging us on. We were used to seeing him, stretched out in his tight worn jeans and a bright colored T-shirt that showed off those arms with the thick blue veins. I can still trace those veins in my mind as if they were roads I've driven on in the midwest. Long and thick and going nowhere.

I'd been with him the summer before, but he never stayed with anyone too long. I had a new boyfriend now, named Hank. Hank picked me up after practice every day and we'd go to Sherman's for hamburgers. Then he'd drive me down to the lake, but I wouldn't let him take me to the places I'd gone to with Bucky.

I knew Bucky well. I knew the only way to have Bucky was not to let him have you. I knew before anybody, because I could tell and because he told me, that Bucky was losing interest in Cindy. I'd heard the rumors about her. How she was hot to trot and had let him cover all the bases. And I wasn't surprised when I heard about Bucky and Sally Sherill.

The first time I heard about it was the night when Hank and I and Bucky and Cindy went cowtipping. First we went to a drive-in, where we polished off a six-pack Bucky had borrowed from his father's liquor cabinet. When the movie got out, Bucky wanted to go cowtipping because he hadn't done it in a while, so we decided why not. There was hardly a better thing to do on a warm summer evening when you'd had some beer than to go cowtipping. We drove out to Libertyville, and while Cindy and I sat on the fence, the boys snuck up on sleeping cows and rammed into them, knocking them over.

Cindy wore yellow shorts and a halter top, and I could see the little beads of sweat on her throat from the warm night. She had long, yellow-tan legs with light yellow fuzz on them and she rubbed them as we sat on that fence. She had a wistful look in her eyes and she took a deep sigh. "I think I've gone and fallen in love with him."

"That's a mistake," I said.

"You aren't jealous, are you?"

I watched as the boys knocked over a few big and startled cows, which tumbled and mooed, their legs in the air like upturned tables. Bucky laughed, flopping on the ground, kicking his legs, and Hank kept trying to lift him up. "Naw," I said, "I'm not jealous. I just don't think you should get messed up with him like that."

Cindy sighed again, rubbing her hands briskly up and down her legs, as if she were trying to make fire. When Bucky had taken up with Cindy, she came over to my house and sat on my bed. "Bucky asked me to a movie."

I'd been seeing Hank since Bucky dropped me the Christmas before, so I said, "Gary's going to be mad."

"What about you?" She'd fiddled with her hair, which was thick and auburn.

I replied, "Oh, he changes every year. You know that." That's how she knew she'd gotten my blessing.

After they woke up the rest of the herd, the boys came back, laughing, in a sweat. "Let's hit the beach," Hank said. Whenever somebody wanted to go to the beach, everyone else knew why. The beach was where we always went to make out, but I didn't want to go now because I'd spent so much time on the beach with Bucky last summer and hadn't been down much since. But that was over, so I said I'd go. We drove down and parked and walked out on the beach.

Bucky walked ahead of us onto the sand. He had assumed his California swagger and was humming "Surfin' " and telling us about this group called the Beach Boys that was the rage out west. He walked down by the shore, his sandy blond hair blowing in the wind, and he paused, taking a deep breath while we caught up with him. When we did, he said, "I hate this lake."

Hank came up behind him. "How can you hate a lake?"

Bucky shrugged. "I just do." He'd always turned up his nose at Lake Michigan since he moved away. It was just a puddle, he'd say. It was nothing. A drop in the bucket. As the summer wore on, Bucky always started longing for the fierce Pacific, where he'd hang ten or drop five. He'd talk about strolling the promenade and about those tall, blond California girls. Then he'd start to look west and get that longing look in his eyes.

Bucky lived with his mother in California, but his father got him for the holidays. He didn't like either of them very much, and what made it worse was that they were his adoptive parents. Bucky used to complain how they'd adopted him and then split. Mrs. Wilson, a big drunk, had taken Bucky away from the icy midwestern winters years ago, and now there was this part of him that couldn't live without the surf.

Bucky and Cindy headed up one end of the beach, and Hank and I went another way. I turned and saw them in the moonlight, Bucky with his arm flapping over Cindy's shoulder, and Cindy giggling, pretending she wanted to get away. I took Hank by the arm and we continued in the opposite direction. After we'd walked a little way, Hank paused and said, "Do you wish you were still with him?"

"I'm glad I'm with you," I said.

"Can you keep a secret?" he asked, putting his arm around my shoulder. He had a catcher's shape, long arms and a crablike torso. He passed his hand through my hair like a whisper. I said I could keep a secret. "Bucky's been hanging out with Sally Sherill." Sally was one of the Highwood gang, and her daddy ran Scofidio's, a favorite bar, and was not somebody you'd want to mess around with. Hank sucked in breath between his teeth. "And you know what they say about her."

A few nights later Bucky called. He called late at night and I grabbed the phone quickly, because I didn't want my mother to get it. He said, "Can you meet me?"

I felt the sweat on my palm as I held the phone. "I don't think so."

But he said, "Don't be a spoilsport. There's a nice moon. I just want to talk to you."

So I slid down my drainpipe, the way I'd done so many nights the previous summer. I walked to the end of my street, where Bucky was waiting with his father's car. He drove down to the lake where we'd always driven and parked the car. When we got out, he tried to take my hand.

I pulled it away and moved close to the water. "I've missed you," he said.

"You could've stayed in touch." I remembered when he'd come back the winter before. He was tan and golden and he hadn't had much time for me. There'd been rumors about him and his stepsister, but I hadn't believed them.

"Anyway, you're with Hank now. He's a nice guy."

I nodded thoughtfully. "He's a nice guy."

We walked a way down the shore and sat on the sand. I felt the damp sand on my legs and the warm breeze off the beach. My hair was back in a ponytail and I let it loose, to let the wind in. He put his arm around me and I sat stiffly beside him. "And you're with Cindy now."

Bucky shrugged. "She's not really my kind."

"You don't know what you like." I sat up straight, my backside pressed into the sand.

"Yes, I do," he said. He turned me around and put his mouth gently to mine. I could feel the moisture of his lips. I pushed him away and said, "I don't want to do this."

But he pulled me back and I could feel the way his lips parted, the way his tongue moved slowly in between the parting lips. His tongue pushed deep down my throat and his hands moved ever so gently up my back. I could feel everything about him. I wondered how I'd forgotten all this. When he slid his hand from my back to my ribs, something jarred me. I sniffed the air. "It stinks down here."

He tried to grab me but I stood up. "Something stinks." I walked to the shore. I put my hand into the water and felt the bodies of some dead fish. I looked where I stood and saw that fish lined the shore. "Dead fish."

Bucky called me back. "Come here. There's always dead fish."

I shook my head. "Not this many. I never saw so many." I looked down at them closely. My father had taught me a lot about fish. "Alewives," I said. "It's all dead alewives."

"What'd you expect? Tuna?" He laughed.

"Strange, it's all one kind." He shrugged and beckoned for me to come back. He didn't know anything about lake fish.

Cindy and I had to make up a biology lab that summer, and the old maid teacher, Miss Guerney, taught us how to pith a frog. She showed us how to bend the head of the frog forward and stick the long needle in and move it around. The frog squirmed and its eyes bulged, but the teacher said the frog didn't feel a thing. She handed out frogs to everyone, but I couldn't bring myself to do the pithing. Cindy and I tried, but the frog just squirmed and then jumped away with the needle sticking in its neck.

After lab Cindy said, "I've got some gossip for you." We went down to the locker room to get ready for practice. Other friends were milling about. "I've heard some stuff," she said. "I heard the boys were over at Sally Sherill's and that she did things to them." I asked Cindy what she did and, with a giggle, she whispered to me something that I couldn't imagine doing to anyone.

After practice was over, Cindy went off with Bucky. He put his hands on her hips and pulled her close to him. The tip of Cindy's breast pressed into Bucky's arm. I wished I'd never gone with him down to the shore.

When Hank came to get me, we went down to the lake to park, but I couldn't bear those pecks like chicken scratchings he put on my neck. After a while I started to squirm and asked him to drop me off. When he did, I blew him a kiss and he looked away, hurt. In the kitchen, my mother kissed me full on the mouth. My father had died a fews years earlier, and my mother was always waiting when I got home. I thought about what Cindy had told me in the locker room and I recoiled from my mother's lips.

A few days later, I stood beside Cindy in the locker room. I looked at her small round breasts, at her smooth skin. I wondered if Bucky had seen as much of her as I had. I could imagine his mouth on her pointed dark nipples. Cindy caught me staring at her, and she looked at me for an instant with a kind of recognition. The night before, she'd come to my house, red-eyed, and we'd gone down to the bluff. "I know," she told me. "I know about him and Sally."

Now, in the locker room, she looked at me again with that same strange look, and it made me think she was capable of anything. "I want to do something," she said. I told her to forget whatever it was she wanted to do. Bucky's no good, I told her. She should go back to Gary. "I know he's no good," Cindy whispered in my ear, "but there's something about him I can't stay away from." She called some of the other girls who were milling around near the lockers. We were going to go over to Marsha's to watch "American Bandstand" and set our hair in hot curlers, something we did a few times a week, but Cindy talked us out of it. She talked us into going to McDonald's, where Sally Sherill worked.

Four of us, including Marsha, a girl named Irene, and me, piled into Cindy's car. We turned the radio on high and put down the top. The Beatles sang, "She Loves You," and we sang along as the car zipped over the Deerfield Road. When we pulled into McDonald's, we could see Sally in her yellow and red striped McDonald's uniform, the stripes expanding across her breasts, as she put French fries and Cokes into McDonald's bags.

When we walked in, Sally smiled tentatively at us. She was a big girl, a dishwater blond with a flat, puglike face and sad brown eyes. "Hi there, Sally," Cindy said.

We lined up along the counter. The place smelled of grease and raw meat. Cindy leaned close to Sally, and Sally smiled now a little uncomfortably. "I'll give you guys some Cokes on the house," she said.

But Cindy waved her hand. "We don't want something for nothing. We've got a proposition for you . . ."

I stepped back a little. The smells of the place were starting to turn my stomach. The Musak grew louder and louder. Sally was smiling.

"We want to make you class treasurer." Sally looked nervous. Her eyes twitched. Cindy paused for great emphasis. "Because we hear you've got the treasure chest."

The girls started to laugh, but I didn't. If I'd had my mother's car, I'd have left. The black kid from Deerfield behind the counter turned away.

Sally looked pale and now her hands were shaking, but she bent forward and leaned into Cindy. "I don't know what your problem is, but you'd better get out of here."

I was halfway to the door. Cindy said, "We know about you. We know a lot."

Sally stepped back, in the direction of the grill, which now had some very well-done cheeseburgers on it. "You'd better get out of here," she said very softly.

"We know about you," Cindy said, turning away from the counter, "and we're gonna tell your daddy, if you don't watch out."

We got back in the car and drove up Sheridan toward Lake Forest. I sat in the back and I couldn't get Bucky out of my mind. I'd tried to get him out, but he was stuck there.

"I want to go home," I said when Cindy started driving north.

"We're going to the beach."

"I don't want to."

Cindy glared back at me; then her face softened with that same look I'd seen in the locker room. She knew she had me. "We'll take you home later. We've got some things to talk over."

I didn't want to talk things over. I just wanted the summer to end and Bucky to go back to where he came from. I wanted to forget how he'd called me almost every night the summer before and how on the nights when he didn't, I'd waited by the phone. Or sat, watching the street sign in front of my house for the headlights of his car. I'd say to myself, I'll wait for six cars, but then six cars would pass and I'd wait for ten cars. I'd spend hours waiting for a car that never came. But then he'd call or come by. And I'd sneak down to the lake to meet him. Bucky always said he had to be close to water. I didn't even like him that much, but I'd always gone.

The whole town started to stink. Nobody knew why the fish were dying, but it just crept up on us. Not all the fish. Just the alewives. They were dying by the thousands. We began staying away from the beach, and it was only mid-July. Everyone began getting restless. One night Marsha had a party when her parents went to Oshkosh for the weekend, and about fifteen of us went over.

We turned down the lights and put on Johnny Mathis. Some wandered away into the yard and a few went upstairs. Hank held me as we danced, his bony arms wrapped around my waist, his nose resting in my neck, and then Bucky cut in. Johnny Mathis was singing "Small World," and I was all wrapped up in Bucky's arms, his hips pressed into mine, his breath on my neck, as if I weren't in this world anymore. I could smell his salt as though he kept the water from the distant coast on his skin the whole time.

I had to get away from that party, so I let Hank take me down by the bluff, where he stood, his back plastered against a tree that he kept kicking with his foot like an angry horse. The moon was full, and from the bluff and for as far as we could see, there were the bodies of dead fish. They lined the shore and were piling up deep into the water. "I knew it," I said. Alewives were stupid fish. Vile, eel-like things. They didn't do anything. They had dumb names that didn't mean anything and they didn't even belong in the Great Lakes in the first place. They'd snuck in, up the St. Lawrence, and turned themselves into freshwater fish. You couldn't even eat them. And when they felt like it, they went and died.

Since we couldn't go to the beach anymore, the cheerleaders started hanging out in Highwood and in the delis in the evenings and after practice. One evening we went to Strike 'n Spare for pizza and to bowl a few rounds. We were having a good time, laughing, when Bucky walked in with Sally.

Cindy didn't notice, because she was bowling, but I did. When Bucky walked by with Sally, her laughter echoed through the bowling alley, striking like a ball smashing the pins. There was something about Sally as she walked through the place. It was in the way she moved and in the scent that seemed to come from her. She made Bucky look as if he were back in California. She had something, I knew then, that none of the rest of us had, and I couldn't help wishing I had it.

A few nights later Cindy did notice. We'd gone to the old Alcyon Theater, where our feet stuck to the floor in caramel and sour butter. We always dipped our hands into each other's popcorn and laughed at the lovers who snuggled in the back. We shouted and shot popcorn rockets at the screen until the ushers tried to toss us out.

But this time we took up our row and never watched the screen. Instead, we watched the second row, where Bucky and Sally and some of the other boys sat. Cindy slowly munched on her popcorn, her eyes fixed on the second row. We watched them doing things to Sally and when they got up and walked back, Cindy poked me in the ribs and I saw Hank, his body ramming against Sally the way he'd rammed the sleeping cows. When they passed us, we whistled. Hank looked at me as though I should've known all along.

I turned to Cindy. "Let's go," I said. We got up in unison. We were maybe eight and we got into our cars and drove swiftly to the beach. In the parking lot, I saw Hank's car. We got out and followed the sound of the water and their muffled voices, and we snuck up on them, real slow. It was a hot July night and the beach just stank of the fish, and the flies swarmed around us and we could see the movement of bodies, like gentle waves, lapping the shore.

Cindy called out first. She said, "Bucky, why don't you go back to California and stay there? We don't need your kind here."

And from somewhere the boys — there were maybe five of them — came forward, as if they'd just walked out of the sea, their bodies all wet and shiny, and Sally was nowhere to be seen. But Hank stood there, acting as if he didn't know me. And then Bucky came up. He walked straight up to us and caught Cindy by the arm. He said, "Why don't you tell them what I did to you, Cindy. Come on. Why don't you tell them. You remember, don't you? You remember what I did."

When Miss Guerney called the meeting, all the girls wanted to know why. We were told to report to Miss Guerney's homeroom one morning in July. Just the girls. I knew why. When Cindy told me she was going to tell, I hadn't told her not to.

We shuffled in the summer heat and in the stink of the beach, which reached all the way to the schoolroom. We lined the back of the classroom and the room was filled and hot. Miss Guerney had bad breath and huge breasts and nobody had ever wanted her and we all drew back when she talked to us because she spit her bad breath in our faces. In the front of the room sat Sally Sherill, and beside her, a tall, stiff gray-haired woman in a trim pink shirtwaist dress. The woman clasped a handkerchief in her fingers and from time to time she pressed it to her eyes.

Miss Guerney told us to be quiet and said that a bad example had been set. She said this bad example needed to be corrected. "There have been rumors and they have gotten back to me." She said that girls had to preserve their bodies and that what one girl had done was bad for everyone.

Then she had the bad girl Sally, wearing a yellow dress, stand up. And Sally stood and told us all. "I've done things," she said, her strong doglike face set firm. "I've done some things I am ashamed of." I felt my head starting to turn from the heat in the room and I watched sweat crawling down people's backs. Some flies buzzed overhead and I could smell the stink the summer had brought. Sally's face started to crack, then shattered in front of us as if somebody had thrown a bottle into glass.

Instead of going right home, I rode to the beach. It was the last time I went down to the lake that summer. Some of the workers who'd volunteered to rake the alewives were burning them in little fires. I walked past the fires of burning alewives, who'd been killed, they said, by lamprey eels that sucked their insides out. I picked up fish by their tails and tossed them over my head. I stripped down to my underwear. One of the workers called out to me, "Hey, what're you doing?" as I swam, the viscous water sticking to me like tar, in the lake I knew so well.

Shining Path

RAMÓN keeps his scorpion close to his heart. He keeps it in a box under his shirt and pulls it out only when he is asking for money. He doesn't show it to his friends anymore. Not since Pablo and Juan stole his rat from him. Now he guards the scorpion, pressing it to his heart.

When Victoria leaves her room in the morning, she heads for Ramón's sand dune. Sometimes she thinks it's a miracle she ever finds his straw hut. There are hundreds, thousands, just like his on the dunes, and the dunes are all alike, stretching for miles. But Victoria's been here enough and she knows. She knows to tell the driver to drop her off across from the fruit stand where the old woman with the blind child sells bruised mangoes and plantains. She walks straight up the dune past ten rows of houses, then she turns left and it is the fourth house. Though sometimes it is the third or the fifth house. It all depends. It depends on what has happened the night before. On who has come or whose house has been washed away by the rain and mud.

Or sometimes the people just disappear. Ramón has told her that you can get up in the morning and the people are gone. They've taken whatever they have and they've taken their straw mats and the cardboard that makes up their house. But sometimes they've left their house behind and sometimes even their belongings. And when this happens, no one ever talks of them again and it is never long before someone else just moves in.

Though she's been to Ramón's house many times, Victoria is always surprised when she gets there. The people know her now and she knows them, but still she's shocked. She hasn't gotten used to the naked children covered with sores, bloody from scratching. Or to the man whose two hands and half his nose were chopped off by a machete in a lover's quarrel. She hasn't even gotten used to the dog who's scratched all the fur off his belly and his testicles and who keeps biting at them.

She kneels down in the dust and finds Ramón asleep in his hut. It has been dry for weeks now and the dune has no caked mud on it. A thin layer of dust coats everyone, everything. It makes Ramón look as if he's dead. It makes everyone look as if he's being buried alive. Ramón's dark smooth skin is coated white. Flies swarm around his eyes, crusty with sleep, and he swats the air in his sleep. He sleeps with the pile of rags he has collected pulled over him. On his brow there is a fine line of sweat, and she can tell he's having a bad dream. But after a few moments he looks up at her, serenely at first, then startled. He is late for work.

He grabs his sponge and bucket and fills the bucket with water from the well. He takes off his ragged T-shirt and puts on another ragged T-shirt. These are the only two shirts he has, and she's never seen him change his pants. He rushes back to the well and throws water on his face and his hands. He's told her that this dune is better than the last dune he lived on because here there is a well.

"Where's Sam?" he asks, wiping his face on his T-shirt.

She tells him Sam is sleeping. He winks at her. "You getting along?"

Ramón has told her at times that he is in love with her, even though she's old enough to be his mother. He has told her he wants to be first in line when she leaves Sam.

They say that when this place was conquered four hundred years ago, Pizarro asked the Inca leader where the best place would be to put his city, the seat of his empire. And the Inca leader showed him this spot by the sea. If you ask the campesinos, they will tell you the Incas played a big joke on the conquerors. You do not have to spend much time here to see why.

It is a desert where nothing will grow. The sea blows hot and humid and it brings no relief. There are no trees, no grass, and when the wind comes down from the sierra, the town is covered in sand. It is not the pale, golden sand of the Arabian deserts. This desert has the dust of a dirt road — a muddy, gray sand — and the people have dusty, gray faces.

Victoria knew all of this before she came here, but she knew nothing of the sky. No one told her until the plane landed that they called it *pelo de burro*, hair of the donkey. They call it that because it is always gray, the gray shade of a donkey's hide, and because it looks overworked and burdened. Sam was depressed when they arrived. He said they should have gone to Mexico or even Haiti. But Victoria is a photographer and she's made her reputation on ugly places.

At the intersection where Ramón works, Victoria finds a spot to sit in the shade. She sits down as he gets his bucket and sponge ready. A few weeks ago someone stole his bucket and he had to save for a week before he had enough money for a new one. He is glad when she comes with him so that she can watch the bucket.

Victoria takes out her notebook and sets up her camera. For the past two weeks she has been photographing Ramón. She could easily have completed her assignment weeks ago, but she decided to do a human interest feature on Ramón. This is one of the things she and Sam argued about the night before. Sam says she's not here to do a human interest piece. She's here to do a travel piece on the *pueblos jovenes.* What they call the young villages. They are called young villages because the people who live here are considered to be moving up in the world. Each village has a well and a small fenced-in sandlot where children can play.

Sam tells her she's spending too much time with Ramón and that she's forgotten what she's supposed to be doing in the first place. Sam may be right, but Victoria doesn't care. She watches Ramón as he prepares his bucket with soapy water. "You know what I want?" he says. "I want a bus. I want to drive my own bus." He has told her this before. He has told her that when the revolution comes, he wants his own bus. For now the revolution is still mostly in the sierra, but Ramón says that when it comes to the city, he wants his own bus. He wrings out the soapy sponge. Then he looks up at one of the hills and smiles. "Last night they took the light away."

She nods. Last night several electric pylons were blown up. Ramón always seems happy when this happens.

"I saw them on the hill with their torches." Then he kisses her on the forehead and dashes into the intersection. He waits for the light to change. When it changes, he jumps on a car that has stopped and quickly soaps down the windshield so that the driver cannot see. If the driver doesn't give him fifty soles, he won't wipe the soap away. Victoria thinks this isn't fair, but he says lots of things in life aren't fair.

If the driver gives him the fifty soles, Ramón sometimes

pulls out the scorpion and sometimes the driver will give him more. He used to stand at the intersections, eating fire. He says he prefers earning his money this way.

The first time Victoria saw Ramón, it was near an old outdoor market on the outskirts of the city. Whenever she gets to a new place, she spends a few days walking around, just to get the feel of it. The day she arrived she went up the hill to the market, which isn't far from the sand dune where he lives. Outside the market, a garbage truck, obviously overloaded, had dropped several carefully wrapped plastic bags that came from the richer parts of the city, where the hotels are. That is the only part of town where they can afford to wrap up their garbage.

She stopped to look. Old men, dogs, and small children were ripping the bags apart, and by the time she got there, everyone was eating. Victoria had done a special on garbage in America, and this was good garbage. She could see that right away. The people and the dogs scrambled in the bags and came up with chicken bones, soggy bread, rancid meat, while women snatched up pieces of cloth to wrap their babies in.

In the midst of this pile, a young boy caught her eyes. He was filthy, but he had deep dark eyes. He clasped a ragged shirt to him, which he later added to his pile of rags, and when no one was looking, he devoured a chicken wing, bones and all. Then he glanced at her, a strange look of contentment in his eyes.

Even though she didn't have her camera with her, the image of him stuck in her mind. The next day when she returned to the market, he was there, almost waiting for her, it seemed.

When Ramón finishes work that day, she heads for Harry's. Ramón says he'll meet her later. He doesn't like

Sam and he doesn't want to see him. Harry's is a fast-food place in Miraflores where they serve good steak and eggs.

When Victoria gets to Harry's, Sam still hasn't arrived, but Harry comes over to her table. "Have you seen Sam?" she asks, and Harry nods. "Left in a huff about an hour ago. I don't know if he'll be back." She shrugs as if she doesn't really care. "I'll catch up with him eventually."

Harry is a Jew who left Germany in 1939. Now, he complains, he's going to have to leave this place as well. Harry is in his sixties, but he wears a denim leisure suit. He combs his thick gray hair forward across his bald spot and lacquers it down with hair spray. He looks like a cockatoo and he is lonely because his wife and three daughters have moved to New York.

When Sam walks in, he pretends he doesn't see her at first. He says hello to Harry. Then he looks surprised to see Victoria. He waves at her, making his hand move in a round motion as if he's polishing glass. She smiles and eats her steak and eggs. It is a huge order and it's more than she can eat. Sam pulls back a chair and sits down. He picks up a piece of the steak, so Victoria motions to the waitress to bring another fork. "Well, they haven't got the lights back in this part of town," he says. She doesn't know why he says this. It's obvious the lights aren't back.

"Did you buy more rugs today?" Sam spends most of his day buying rugs and handicrafts. He has a partner on the West Coast and they want to open a boutique.

He ignores her question. "Ready to go to Mexico?" He runs his fingers through her hair.

"I need a little more time with Ramón. I wanta make sure I've got a day in his life."

Sam nods. He's heard the same line for the past two weeks. "I suppose I should be jealous."

She shakes her head at him. "Don't be ridiculous."

Sam chews on a T-bone. "So why're you taking so long?

You've always just been in and out of these places before."

Victoria shrugs and runs her fork through the egg yolk. She's not sure she herself knows what the difference is. It was a few years ago when she came up with the idea as a joke, and her magazine thought it was a great notion, something no one had done before. Victoria suggested doing travel pieces on ugly places where nobody wants to go. On burned-out fishing villages in Mexico, on flea-bitten towns in North Africa, on the slums of major cities. She was surprised when the idea caught on. Victoria is now the world's leading expert on places nobody wants to visit.

When she proposed the slums of Lima, some people on her magazine were thrilled. Among the well informed, the slums of Lima are the best, or the worst, depending on which way you look at it. Until now these trips have always worked out for Victoria and Sam, because while Victoria visits ugly places, Sam buys for the shop he plans to open. But on this trip Sam has been jittery since they got here. He points to Harry and leans forward. "He told me nobody's changing money. He says all the tourists are leaving."

Victoria rubs her eyes. They bother her because of the exhaust from the cars on the intersection where Ramón works. "We're not tourists."

"Listen, they're very organized," he says in a low voice. "Do you know that last night all eight pylons were blown simultaneously? All at once. Like clockwork."

"Sam, if you want to leave, you can. I don't want to keep you here."

"I could never leave you, baby." He gives her a kiss on the forehead. "I just wanta get you out of town."

That night, as they're making love, Victoria gazes out the window. She sees two dark eyes staring in. She thinks it is Ramón, coming to tell her something, so she jumps out of bed and, rushing to the window, flings it open. No one is there, or if anyone was there, he's gone. Sam lies with his head flung back against the pillow, arms shielding his face. "Vicky, what're you doing?" he says. And then "Come back to bed."

The next night Victoria and Sam take Ramón to a hamburger joint for dinner. They order good American food — hamburgers, fries, Cokes. They sit by the window and, while street urchins press their noses to the glass and rub their stomachs, talk about how good it feels to eat hamburgers. Ramón chews slowly, his eyes darting constantly from Victoria to Sam. He is always almost silent around Sam. Victoria has to sit with her back to the window in order to eat and Sam keeps shooing the children away, but they keep their noses pressed to the window.

Ramón has brought her a picture. It is a picture of dogs hanging by ropes from trees. He points to the picture and tells her that they are hanging the dogs up in the sierra. They have hanged dogs in other revolutions, Ramón tells her, so why shouldn't they hang dogs in this one. He tells her he has seen the dogs hanging. They twist and yelp and sometimes they take a long time to die. She puts her hand to her throat and thinks that if you gave her a choice, she'd rather die quickly at thirty than slowly at eighty.

Victoria looks at Ramón, who has cleaned himself up for this occasion. He is wearing a shirt he must have borrowed or stolen from someone. His jet-black hair is slicked back, and the white dust has been removed from his skin. Victoria wonders how she'll tell him when she's leaving. She'd like to say to him "I'll write you," but it's difficult to write to someone who lives on a sand dune.

When they leave the hamburger joint, Victoria feels stuffed, disgusted with herself. There is the taste of oil in her mouth. They pass peasant women, their breasts exposed, begging and pointing to crying children. The women are saying their breasts have dried up and they have nothing to feed their babies. Ramón looks at the women, but they seem to bother him, and he walks on. So does Sam. But Victoria stops. She gives each of the women a hundred-soles piece. When she catches up with Sam, he is annoyed. He says, "You're not going to save the world that way."

When they pass Harry's, Sam goes in to order a beer while Victoria says good-bye to Ramón. Something has made him gloomy, so she bends to kiss him on the cheek, but he seems to be listening to something. She listens too and then she hears it. She hears crickets, chirping in the night, and she smiles. "I love crickets," she tells him.

But he shakes his head. "I don't. They make me sad. They make me think about something I don't want to think about." Then he tells her about one night when he was a little boy and he was tending sheep in the sierra. He says, "A jaguar ate one of the lambs and the people I worked for were angry with me. So they wouldn't give me any food for a day. That night I stayed awake and I couldn't sleep because I was so hungry. And all night long I listened to the crickets chirping." Then he looks at her firmly, almost angry. "And I swore I'd never be hungry again. Whenever I hear the crickets, that's what I think. I think how I'll never be hungry again."

The night the terrorists blow up the electric company, Victoria is getting a manicure in the Turkish baths. She usually gets a massage or a manicure on Friday nights because there isn't much else to do in this place on weekends; most of the clubs and theaters are on the hit list. But lately they've been bombing the electric company on Friday nights. They'd skipped a few Fridays, and since Sam and she aren't talking much these days, she thought this might be a good evening for the Turkish baths.

As the lights begin to fade, women grab their towels and scramble around. In the dark, the smell of eucalyptus from the sauna is sharp and makes her think of soothing, tropical nights. In the fading light, she can see the shiny backsides of women as they dash, scrambling for their clothes, laughing or cursing, annoyed with the inconvenience. The manicurists and masseuses look for candles. Victoria's manicurist finishes her feet by candlelight. It isn't until the next morning that she notices the manicurist's thumb print, neatly embedded in the polish of her nail. She could probably run a security check on her with that alone.

She leaves the baths, fed up with the blackouts and power failures, but this night it's a little different. The streets are as dark as they've ever been, but police cars scour them, sirens piercing the night. In front of her a newsstand is in flames, burning to the ground. As she rides home in the colectivo, she sees other newsstands burn while stores with broken windows are being robbed. She's never seen newsstands on fire before.

She goes back to the apartment to look for Sam. The place is pitch black, and she is surprised to find him not there. When she lights a candle, she finds instead a note on the kitchen table. It reads, "This is some vacation. If you want to join me, I'll be at the Poc-Na on Isla Mujeres." Sam knew from the start that it wasn't going to be a vacation. Victoria spends the night alone in the dark, waiting for Sam to return, but he doesn't. A few times in the night she thinks she hears a sound in the hallway, and she jumps up, shouting, "Sam? Is that you?" In the morning, when the sunlight comes in, she feels better. She is surprised that he actually had the nerve to leave, but in the daylight it doesn't really worry her so much. She figures she'll catch up with him back home.

The next afternoon Victoria has to go to the embassy to get her visa renewed. She's also trying to get a pass to go into the sierra, even though she knows that the sierra isn't part of her assignment at all. As she walks by, there is a demonstration in front of the embassy, and she stops to watch it. About a hundred students carry banners. Some wear costumes. One is the Big Bad Wolf with U.S.A. on his chest, gobbling a basket of goodies labeled CENTRAL AMERICA. Another is Uncle Sam, but as a skeleton. As cars pass, the drivers honk. At first she thinks they are honking because the students are blocking traffic, but the honking is too rhythmic, too systematic. It is almost like tribal drums she once heard on the Honduran border.

She goes into the embassy, where the embassy people are walking around with their hands over their ears. The honking has been going on for a few days. They say it grows louder and louder and the police can't seem to make it stop. The honking is driving some embassy officials mad. An official she's been dealing with tells her he is sorry but he cannot get her any special permits and he doesn't advise her to renew her visa. He says, off the record, "We think it would be better if you leave." Then he confides in her, "A kind of torpedo, filled with dynamite, was shot into the embassy courtyard yesterday. Didn't go off, but it could have." White saliva is in the corners of his mouth as he speaks, and his hands tremble.

In the evening she decides she needs to find Ramón. She goes to his usual places. She goes through Miraflores and down in front of Harry's. It's too early for him to return to his sand dune. He'd still be working the streets. He is, in fact, near Harry's, begging for money. He is dirtier than usual. His hair is matted, his clothes shredded. He clasps his scorpion close to his heart. She waves him over and he comes, smiling, showing her a fistful of money he's already begged that night. "You're a mess," she says.

"Nobody gives me a thing if I'm clean," he answers with a laugh.

"What's going on," she asks, somewhat somberly.

"Same as always," he replies, taking her arm. He points to the hill that overlooks the city, the hill where the police won't go. The night before, he tells her, he saw torches in the shape of a hammer and sickle. "Only this time it's a little bit more."

Then he says, "I have to talk to you, but not here." He takes her by the arm and leads her down the street to a block where some of the light has been restored. It is a gray, cloudy night, and great humidity hangs in the air. He leans his face close to hers and whispers, "When you get back home," he says, "you're going to tell your paper about all of this."

She nods. She tells him she's going to tell her paper about all of it.

Then he says, "Listen, something is going to happen here. Something very big."

"What? What's going to happen?"

He shakes his head. "I'm not sure. It's just that there's been a lot of talk. You should leave," he tells her.

She thanks him for the warning. "Sam left," she tells him.

Ramón smiles. He is just a boy, no more than fifteen. He reaches up and cups his hands around her face. He holds her face in his hands and runs his hands over her cheeks. She feels as if he is looking at something as distant and bright as the moon, but it's just her face. She feels the calluses on his hands; they're coarse, like animal paws. He puts his mouth close against hers. "Take me with you," he says. "When you leave" — his mouth is very close to hers and she can feel his breath — "when you leave, take me."

She stares into his eyes and he stares back into hers. His eyes are bright and filled with a kind of fire, which she realizes is coming from the streetlight behind her, but they give him an unreal light. He grips his hands tighter around her head and she shakes her head in his hands. He brings his lips to hers. His lips feel chapped, but his mouth is wet and warm. Victoria pulls back. "I can't," she says. "I can't take you with me."

She starts to explain, but he steps back. He wipes the back of his hand across his mouth and walks away.

The next evening Victoria goes for a massage at the baths. The masseuse rubs hot oil and salt on her hands and tells her that she had to flee Argentina ten years ago and now she thinks she'll have to leave again. Victoria's muscles seem to stiffen more and more, no matter how much the masseuse tells her to relax. She has her hands pressed firmly around Victoria's neck when the lights go off. Victoria thinks of the picture of the hanging dogs Ramón showed her.

She dresses in the dark and heads out into the night, looking for him. He will tell her what's going on. She wanders the streets, looking for him, but she doesn't find him and she can't find a cab to take her to his sand dune. She notices that this time, for some reason, the city seems darker. It is strange that it's so quiet. There are no cars honking, no sirens piercing the night. There is no smell of burning nor the sound of shouting. It's too quiet, she thinks. It's as quiet as a country road in Vermont. A city this size should never be that quiet, and certainly not after bombs have gone off. The people who walk the streets do not look afraid, but their faces are dark and quiet as the night.

That night Victoria drinks a glass of brandy to help her sleep. She lets a candle burn and some time in the night she feels the candle go out. Cold air blows down her neck. As she moves in and out of sleep, she thinks someone is touching her hair. She dreams someone is putting his lips to her cheek. Her legs feel a chill. When she wakes at dawn, stretching like someone who has just made love, she realizes she has no covers on. Except for her T-shirt, she is naked. As she reaches for the covers, she feels the draft from the open window. She sees her clothes, lying all over the floor. It takes her another moment to assess the situation. Her eyes scan the room, looking for something, but she's not sure what. It takes a while longer for it to sink in. Her camera is gone from the top of the dresser. So is all her film.

She dresses quickly and hails a cab to take her to the sand dune. Her heart pounds as the taxi zips through the deserted streets where no lights shine. She climbs the dune, up ten rows, and across four. She walks along the row where his house is, past the sick people, past the dog biting at his testicles, past the man with no hands who lost them for love. She walks back and forth but doesn't find Ramón's house of straw.

Victoria retraces her steps, certain this is the right dune because the old woman with the blind child was selling her mangoes at the foot of it. She's certain she counted ten rows up and over four. What she does find is a young woman with two small children, living inside a house of straw where Ramón's should have been. Or maybe it was Ramón's house. She can't tell; they all look alike.

She asks the woman about him and the woman laughs. She's fat, with missing teeth, and she holds out a withered hand, asking for money. Victoria gives her the change in her pocket and the woman points across the dunes, into the sierra, but from where Victoria is standing, all she can see is more dunes. Dust settles on her skin. She doesn't wipe it away.

Summer Share

THE HOUSE is the same as I remember it. Still white and set back from the road. The pink and purple rhododendrons still flower, first the pink, then the purple. I go into the back porch and find the key, which is in the same place where we've left it, under the second flower pot. It always seemed like such an obvious place that no thief would look there. I am the first to arrive, and it is my job to open the house.

When I walk in, my first weekend this summer, I can tell that someone else has recently been here. A cup of coffee sits in the sink, and when I go upstairs to put down my things, there is the imprint of a body on my bed. I take the same bed as last year and the year before that and before that. The bed I shared with Robert. I smooth out the imprint on my bed, which feels almost cold. It is not Robert's. It is as if an old woman or a child has lain down here. Or perhaps a dog. But a dog wouldn't make coffee for itself.

By the time I return from the fish store, Marilyn and Jed are sitting in the lawn chairs, sipping lemonade. Jed is talking about Sally, the woman he was with in the house last year. "She wasn't anything like Francesca," Jed says. "Was she, Patsy?" Nobody in my whole life except Jed calls me Patsy. Though I've tried for the past three summers to have him call me Patricia, he won't. I've learned to live with this as I've learned to live with other things in the house.

Cindy arrives a little later and goes to work on the garden. It's really her garden, even though we've all tried at times to lend a hand. Cindy planned how much we could plant and cut the garden back almost to the potato field. She's the one who put the marigolds between the rows and who empties the dishes of beer we leave out to kill the slugs.

Cindy gets the hose and begins to go to work. It's a week since anyone has done anything, and yet in the middle of her weeding she pauses. "The garden's been weeded," she says. "Somebody weeded it."

"Naw," Jed says, "you just did an extra good job last weekend."

"I don't know." Cindy sticks her finger in the soil. "It's been watered too."

"The guy who cuts the lawn probably did it," I suggest.

She tucks the hose under a zucchini plant. "I think I'd like to be a horticultural therapist."

"What's that?" Jed says. "You help the plants work out their growth problems, need for space and attention?"

Cindy looks at him and frowns. "You're a jerk. You help people work out their problems through working with plants. It's very nurturing."

"Must be a big field." Jed laughs. Nobody gets it for a few minutes. Then we groan. Jed and I go into the kitchen to start dinner. He opens the fish I've bought and sniffs it, holding the fish up to the light. "What's this?"

"Flounder," I say, watching him stick his nose into the fish.

"Flounder should be gray, not blue. It's spoiled."

I shrug. I did take my time getting back. I took the long way, past the horse farms near the beach, the way we always liked to go. "They said it was fresh."

"Stinks." Jed is a bit of a gourmet, but he'll make do. He washes the fish and rubs it carefully with lemon and garlic. It still smells fishy and now some of it has turned from blue to a suspect shade of green. "We won't tell them," he mutters. "They'll never notice."

Arthur comes in time for dinner, and we're all a little disappointed. Arthur is a chain smoker and he never lets a meal go by without getting into a heated discussion about U.S. imperialism. Arthur is planning a trip to Nicaragua, and none of us is trying to dissuade him from going. Arthur has brought his girlfriend, Angeline. This is totally unexpected, though he swears he cleared it with Jed. Jed is in charge of guests, and all guests must be cleared.

My room has always been my room, the large master bedroom in the front, but then I always shared that room with Robert. We liked that room because it had bigger windows and was far away from the bathroom. It's true you have to pass through the big bedroom to get to the little bedroom, so there's not much privacy, but we managed.

"I guess I'll move into the little room," I offer.

But Arthur won't hear of it. "No, it's your room." He holds up the schedule as if it were the Bill of Rights. "We'll stick to our schedule."

"I really don't care," I go on, but he won't hear of it. Then I think of it. "Someone's slept on top of my bed."

Jed shrugs. "Maybe someone stayed out last week."

"No one stayed out," I say; I know because scheduling is my task.

"And the garden's been weeded," Cindy mentions.

"Maybe it was Goldilocks." Arthur giggles.

"And there was a cup of coffee in the sink."

"Well, that could've been left," Jed begins. But I cut in: "It was fresh coffee."

"I'll talk to the realtor," Marilyn says, since she always deals with the realtor, and we leave it at that.

We sit down to a candlelit dinner of flounder and pasta. Arthur has surprised us by bringing four kinds of pie. Blueberry, cherry, rhubarb, and peach. He lines them all up on the sideboard beneath the picture of the woman who lived in the house fifty years ago. Her eyes follow us around in the dining room as if she's making sure we're taking care of things.

Arthur is plump and smokes between courses; Cindy waves the smoke away with her hand. "I don't think people should be allowed to smoke in the house," she says, but everyone ignores her. Arthur's smoking drives Cindy mad, but we can't do anything about it. He's got seniority over everyone but me, so unless we all decide to get rid of him next year, there isn't much we can do about him.

Cindy's the one who's allergic to everything. She made us purchase spring water because she says she's allergic to the pesticides that have sunk into the water table. She won't let me put Open Pit Barbecue Sauce on the special barbecued chicken I make almost every Saturday. I have to cook her chicken on a separate part of the grill, but sometimes I cheat and give her a piece with Open Pit on it, and so far she's never been able to tell the difference.

"So, how d'ya like the fish?" Jed asks Arthur.

"Delish," Arthur replies, pulling a bone from his mouth.

Jed looks at me and winks. "You like flounder." Arthur nods and keeps eating. Jed starts to talk about how when he lived in Mexico his maid made this great fish with garlic and green olives.

Arthur begins to boil. "Hope you paid her minimum."

"I did," Jed says, "for there."

"What's that? Two cents a day?" Jed is an account executive for a large insurance firm, and though he's a good cook, he is, according to Arthur, a lousy person. Not that he isn't a nice person. He's your average nice, considerate person, and that's all that really matters for a summer share. But Jed has no conscience, according to Arthur, who works for a public interest law firm. Whenever they are out on the same weekend, we just hope we can get through dinner without an argument.

We can't. They begin to argue. Jed says he was giving a poor person a job, and Arthur says so do multinationals in the Third World. Cindy can't stand conflict, so she begins to do the dishes. I talk to Marilyn about an auction being held the next day. But then I decide I am tired and want to go to sleep. "Excuse me," I say, "but do you want me to move into the small room?"

Arthur won't hear of it, though Angeline bumps him in the arm. "We'll sleep outside," Arthur offers. "We've got our sleeping bags." Angeline doesn't want to sleep outside; that's clear. She makes a joke about getting AIDS from mosquitoes, which no one thinks is very funny.

"I hate it when people sleep outside," Cindy says as she clears the table, but she doesn't say why.

I go upstairs to go to bed and find that the imprint on the bed is still there, though I distinctly remember having smoothed it out.

There's a bird who lives in the roof somewhere, and he drives me crazy. He makes a terrible sound that no bird should make and he wakes me at five in the morning. I've heard him before, but this morning he seems louder than usual. His sound isn't a chirp or a song. Rather, it's a relentless call, repeated over and over.

I get up to see if I can locate the bird and maybe throw a beach clog at him or something. Down in the yard I see Arthur, the revolutionary with four kinds of pie in him,

going at it with Angeline, who's afraid of intimate contact
with mosquitoes. The top of the sleeping bag rises and falls,
and Arthur's plump backside moves up and down.

The bird finally stops, but I can't go back to sleep. I
should have insisted on sleeping in the little room, though
I'm not sure I could have handled anyone else sleeping in
our bed. But the backyard was our territory too. We'd
staked it out long ago, one weekend, when Robert and I
had the house to ourselves. It was a cool, green summer's
night with an orange moon, and we went outside to check
on the vegetables. It was a cloudless night, and I remember it perfectly because Robert dropped his head back and
said, "God, look at those stars." Then he pulled a beach
towel off the line and stretched it on the ground. "We
should stay outside. Here. We should lie down and look."

I stay in bed until late in the morning. When I finally get
up, I stumble down into the den and find Marilyn rum-
maging through the locked closet. "What're you doing?"
I'm somewhat aghast. The locked closet has always been
the locked closet.

Marilyn shrugs. "I found the key."

"We're not supposed to go in there. You know that."

But Marilyn has surrounded herself with memorabilia.
"Look what I found." She shows me tiddlywinks and
pickup sticks, pinochle, and some card game we can't figure out, all from about 1934. She shows me a stack of
photographs. Some of these things I've seen before, but
there are other things I haven't.

Marilyn plunks something down in front of me. I see a
leather-bound book, and I open it up. It is somebody's
postcard collection. It's much older than the games, and
we flip through slowly, removing some of the cards to read
what's written on the back. They are from all over the
world. From Africa and South America, from the United
States and Europe, from China and Japan. I see a statue
of a rhino in front of the Eiffel Tower; the card reads,

"Edie, you must visit this tower. It's completely ridiculous." Or "Dearest, we are traveling through the Sudan, but the heat is becoming unbearable. I'll write more from the Nile delta, where, we're told, it will be cooler. All our love."

All the cards are addressed to Edie. We know who Edie is. She is Richard's wife. Edie is the mother of the man, Mr. Wendell, who owns the house. It is Edie's picture that is above the mantel in the dining room. Richard and Edie have been dead for many years, and Alex Wendell has been renting to us for the past five years. We find it strange that Alex has left behind so many of his parents' things. Last year, for instance, we found a photograph of Edie and Richard in which Richard was stooped over with, we learned from a neighbor, some rare disease.

I've gone through some of the memorabilia before on my own. I've used the old sewing kit to fix a blouse and in the garage I've sat on the rocking horse that Richard carved out of wood. The garden supplies we use are antiques, and the man at the hardware store laughed at me when I came in with a scythe I wanted sharpened.

I feel odd as I go through the postcard collection, and finally I tell Marilyn, "We'd better put this stuff away."

That night I wake up and feel certain I'm not alone. I feel someone lying beside me. There's a warmth to the bed, and I can hear breathing, even, next to me. I think that I should be terrified, but for some reason I'm not. Instead, I'm oddly comforted. After a few moments, just as it begins to get light, I reach out and I feel a blank space, colder than any empty space should be.

In the morning I go to the store to buy things we need, like toilet paper and sugar. Cindy is in the kitchen as I unpack the groceries. She picks up the Charmin. "What's this?"

I say, "It's four rolls of Charmin."

"Do you plan to take it back to the city with you?"

So I say no, I think we'll use it in the course of the summer, but she shakes her head. "Perfume," she says. "It's got perfume in it. You should only buy Scott. No perfume in Scott. Do you mind if I return this?"

"You're gonna return toilet paper? Sure, return it."

I'm heading out the door. "Oh, by the way," Cindy says, "I meant to tell you. I ran into Robert on the bus. I guess he's got a place in Water Mill this summer."

"Oh," I say, moving closer to the door.

"He looked good." She smiles. "Nice and tan." She's trying to figure out why I'm not asking more questions about Robert. "He said to say hello."

"Thanks," I mutter and walk into the yard.

I get my bike out of the garage and take the road to the shore. I ride with the breeze from the potato field blowing through my hair. I've told myself the same story many times now. How Robert and I never had a ghost of a chance. How it wasn't meant to be. But for some reason it's never occurred to me that he is out here, going to other beaches. That he is simply going on while I somehow seem to have stopped. I remember everything vividly, though I've tried hard to forget. I remember us jogging in the morning to the beach, holding hands. How we raced for the water. Or getting tipsy in the outdoor shower. The vines of the vineyard covering our heads like a quilt, the amber light from the candle shimmering on ripened grapes. I keep thinking as I ride how these things should be fading, but each moment is as clear as if it had happened the night before.

I ride my bike past the pond where the swans crane their necks and even lift their great fat white bodies off the surface of the water and fly, those same swans we tossed bread to the summer before. I want to look at the swans and think "Those are nice swans," not "Those are the swans I fed with Robert last year."

I feel as if the devil has entered me. It is not something

I say lightly. As if something has found its place in my body and is taking over. In a way it's as if I am never alone. I have this thing living inside me. When I spoke to Robert on the phone last month about picking up some of my things, it sounded as if something had died inside him. Yet in me it lives. It has a life of its own. I feel that if I let it, it could occupy my entire being.

When I get back to the house, Jed and his friends are playing badminton and they're taking up the backyard. Marilyn is painting a picture of the magnolia tree in the front yard, and I sit down next to her in a chair and ask her what the plans are for dinner. She tells me that Cindy is going to eat the fifteen leftover ravioli from last weekend, Arthur is going to a Thai restaurant in Sag Harbor, and Jed is having his badminton partners for dinner and we aren't invited. "We aren't invited? In our own house?" She shrugs. We both know that this has never happened before. We decide to go to the Busy Bee.

It is Sting Hour at the Busy Bee when we get there, and everyone is getting two for the price of one. The tables are crowded, so we start at the bar. A guy comes over and introduces himself to us as "Eric, in advertising," and we introduce ourselves accordingly. When Marilyn tells Eric she's in charge of New York City bat patrol, he's interested but cautious. She explains to him how bats carry rabies, so she has to go to abandoned buildings and find the bats. "Bats don't hang out on Park Avenue, you know." Actually, Marilyn is a fairly accomplished biologist, and the bat patrol is just a sideline. Usually it is good for conversation openers or stoppers. In this case, it's a stopper, and Eric quickly moves on to the next.

When he walks away, Marilyn shrugs. "Men," she says. "Who needs 'em."

The waitress seems to keep bringing us two of everything. We drink vodka tonics, then wine. We gobble down

cheeseburgers and a few more glasses of wine and head out
into the night. It is warm and misty, and the moon seems
hidden behind clouds, but Marilyn tells me it is the best
week of the year to see shooting stars, so we flop down on
the wet grass in a field and stare at the sky, and occasion-
ally, in a clear spot, we do see a star shoot by. "Cindy ran
into Robert on the bus," I tell her during a pause in meteorite activity.

Marilyn sits up. "I was never crazy about you guys together. I don't think he was for you."

I sit up too. "I thought I'd be married by now."

"So did all of us." Marilyn puts an arm on my shoulder. "Maybe it's just a quirk of history. Like being born
before the invention of penicillin or being in Poland in
1939."

We are silent again. "We need massive amounts of love,"
I say.

Marilyn pats my hand. "It's like dependency on foreign
oil." We're both drunk. She continues, "We should be able
to live alone, even if we don't want to." I nod, but I know
I don't want to live alone. I want to pursue this matter in
greater depth, but before I'm able to, Marilyn leaps up and
swears we'll see more shooting stars from the beach, and
for reasons that remain obscure, I believe her.

We get a ride with a potato truck and lie in the back,
potatoes rubbing into our legs, bruising our spines. I am
surprised at how tough these potatoes are. Sturdy Long Island potatoes. I put one in my pocket for good luck. We
wave at the farmer as he drops us off on a black strip of
beach. The beach looks dubious. The moon is hidden behind moving clouds. The ocean is black, except for a mist
that seems to be coming in. We take off our shoes and socks
and leave them near the road and walk out barefoot on
the beach.

I follow Marilyn's lead down to the water. When we get

there, she says, "Come on, let's bury each other." I don't feel like being buried, but she is adamant, and I'm in no shape to argue. We furrow out little graves and then we sit in them, awaiting burial. Slowly we pour sand back over each other until we're covered to the waist. It takes much longer than I had imagined. I'm tired when we finish, and I don't like the cold dampness of the sand. "So now what do we do?"

Marilyn shrugs. "Just sit, I guess."

I'm sitting looking at a pitch-black sea with my legs buried in sand, and Marilyn starts talking about giant squids. She says that up until recently they haven't found any squids alive. They've found them dead, she says, at up to ninety feet, but not alive. Marilyn says they find them attacking ships, but the question has always been why a squid would attack a ship. It's not going to eat the ship. So what's it doing? Marilyn claims to have figured it all out. The giant squids live in the coldest waters of the ocean. If something happens to stir up the water, they're forced to rise to the surface. But when they get into warmer water, their blood boils. You can't imagine what that must feel like, she tells me. So when the water gets stirred up and the giant squids come up to the top of the water, their blood is boiling. That's why they clutch on to the ships. "Because they're in agony." She sighs. "They're in agony."

I stare into the ocean and think that I did unimaginable things near the end to keep Robert from going. Once I blocked the door with my naked body, and even when he threatened to hit me, I didn't move away. I pleaded with him, wrapped my arms around his knees. Suddenly I'm standing up, sand dribbling down my legs, leaving behind my little grave, tears in my eyes. Marilyn leaps up and runs after me. "Hey," she says, "did I do something wrong?"

I shake my head. I tell her I made a mistake. I should've

gone somewhere else this summer. "Robert and I," I tell her, "we had something."

I'm not sure how we got home or how I got into bed. I don't remember taking my clothes off and putting on my nightgown. I'm pretty sure I passed out. I'm wakened when it is still dark by a tapping at the window. I look out and in the moonlight I see a branch, banging in the wind against the windowpane. I stumble out of bed, still half asleep, to open the window and break off the tip of the branch. As I move closer, the branch begins to take on a new form in the moonlight, and just as I reach the window the branch does a strange thing. It beckons to me. It seems to shape itself into fingers on a withered hand and seems to want me to let it in.

I've had other strange dreams since Robert moved out, so this one doesn't surprise me, but I can't go back to sleep. The mattress of my bed, the bed I shared with Robert, is old, and even though we'd put a bed board under it, I can't get comfortable. I remember when I just used to slip into the curve of his back. I'm not sure how I ever slept in this bed before.

I go downstairs and sit in the rocker in the dining room. I feel as if I'm not alone, and when I look up, the eyes of the picture above the mantel seem to be watching me. I look back at Edie Wendell, the woman who owned this house and who kept the postcard collection, and I wonder if she doesn't miss what she's left behind.

I decide to check the vegetables to see how they're doing. I grab a flashlight from the back porch and, standing in the garden in the dark, I shine the light on them. They seem to have grown during the night. The zucchini look bigger than before. The little snow peas have stretched their tendrils farther along the vine. My flashlight finds the beer dishes, and inside dead or drowning slugs stagnate in a murky, viscous solution.

I move the light away, along the ground, and see something fat and thick and pink, pulsating. It is wet and it moves with great enthusiasm. Two earthworms are making love, and they are engrossed for a moment, but the light of my flashlight startles them and they shoot back into their separate holes. I stand dead still in the garden for an instant, catching my breath.

Robert is standing behind me. He has come to check the garden. I can feel him the way I felt him the night we watched the stars. He is so close, I can just reach out and touch him. I tell myself to turn around slowly, but as I do I hear the rustle of leaves, the sound of the wind, and inexplicably he is gone.

When I get back to bed, I see the impression the body has left on the bed. This time I don't bother to smooth it out. This time I let my head slip into the mark on the pillow. I let my legs fold into the creases made by the legs. And when I have fitted myself completely into this impression, this hollow carved-out place, I am finally able to go to sleep. I don't know how long I am asleep when I hear a call of the bird who drives me wild and feel a strange breeze blowing through the room. Though no one is holding me, I feel as if I'm being held.

In the morning I wake to the smell of coffee and wander downstairs. Jed sits at the dining room table, working on the finances with his calculator, and Cindy is adding up the grocery slips.

Jed says, "Patsy, did you take money for briquets out of petty cash?" I haven't even had my coffee yet, so it takes me a moment to understand what he means. I nod yes. Jed says, "Well, briquets aren't like toilet paper. They're individual, not house. So you owe petty cash $5.73, but everyone owes you $2.07." He pauses, perplexed, then annoyed, realizing that he's going to have to redo his calculations because I charged briquets to petty cash.

Cindy looks up. "Be sure you don't charge me for coffee. I'm only drinking tea."

"What about these calls to Tulsa?" Jed asks. "Nobody knows anyone in Tulsa."

Jed gives up on house finances and begins reading the stock reports. Cindy does sit-ups and Marilyn is making eggs. Arthur and Angeline are occupying the living room, engrossed in the paper. Nobody notices me as I walk through the room, but I pause and look at them. They seem strange to me. Though they're only one day older, I can see the difference from the day before. I'm in my swimsuit now, and I move past them, invisible as I float through the house.

Copies

BEVERLY stands at the model 2200, wondering why Doug hasn't looked at her all day. Doug, the man Beverly has been dating for the past six weeks, is busy at the color Xerox. He is her third boyfriend this year. That is one less boyfriend than last year, but it is still more than she wants.

Beverly always meets her boyfriends on the job. She met Andy, the one before Doug, at the Actors' Hotline, where they sat side by side, answering the phone for other people who were getting jobs. One day Beverly answered a call and handed the phone to Andy. "It's for you," she said. It was a producer he'd met at a party a long time ago who had found just the right part for him, and he moved to L.A. in a matter of days. A week after he moved he sent her a postcard of the hills of Hollywood, saying he knew she'd get there some time.

Beverly met Doug after working at the copy center for a few hours. He is a tall, skinny Columbia dropout who is "trying to find himself" and who sits at the edge of her bed at night, playing the guitar while she sleeps. Beverly learned to sleep through anything when she was a little girl and lived with her parents in a small split-level just beyond the northeast approach runway at LaGuardia. Her father wasn't a pilot but a sales representative for a shoe company, and she hardly ever saw him.

Beverly hates the 2200 because there is nothing to do but watch and make certain it doesn't break down. The 2200 can print a hundred pages a minute. When it breaks down, it is a disaster. The Ektaprint is much better than the 2200, but Doug always works on the Ektaprint. Her favorite machine is the binder. She likes the way the frayed edges of paper fall like confetti into the little pouch at the back of the machine. Beverly collects this confetti. She plans to give a party when she leaves the copy center and toss these bits of paper into the air.

It is a Monday morning and there is already a long line of customers with numbers in their hands, waving them at the people who work behind the pale oak counter that separates customer from employee. They wave their tickets as if they were seeing people off who are about to depart on a long cruise. The copy center is done in California-style oak paneling with neatly painted signs that read EXPRESS PICKUP or TAKE A NUMBER, PLEASE. When Beverly came to work here six months ago, she thought it must be a very orderly place, but it isn't very orderly at all.

A nervous homosexual has already been in to complain about the quality of the copies of his last teleplay. Every Monday he comes in to have something copied. He always refuses to drop it off, and sometimes he will wait an hour. Usually he wants thirty copies of everything, done by hand, collated, bound, with a two-tone cover. He is a tedious client, and Doug gets his jobs. But it is Robert, the store manager, who listens to the complaints.

Andrea, Beverly's friend and the assistant manager of the store, is crazy about Robert, but Beverly doesn't see why. Robert is a pale man with stringy brown hair and jagged buck teeth. He is one hundred percent Italian, and Andrea, who studied Italian literature for a term at Pomona College, thinks he is passionate. But Beverly finds him dull and self-absorbed; she thinks the only time Robert ever seems to react to anything is when Mrs. Grimsley comes into the store.

Mrs. Grimsley is an old Irish lady who always thinks other people are butting in line in front of her. She thinks that somehow people can slip a number in between hers and the one they are currently attending to. Mrs. Grimsley writes novels. She once brought in a copy of a novel that survived Hurricane Agnes. The novel was water-stained, the ink was smeared. It was virtually illegible. She told Robert she wanted it copied so that it would become legible.

Robert always gets a headache when he sees Mrs. Grimsley, because Mrs. Grimsley wants the impossible. She wants things made bigger so that she can read them with her failing eyesight, but Robert has explained to her many times that he can't make a page bigger. Mrs. Grimsley doesn't understand. She wants things darker than they are in reality. She wants fingerprint smudges, water stains, ink blotches, removed from the page. She wants her copies to come out perfect.

Mrs. Grimsley had a son who looked just like Robert. He was killed in one of the wars before Robert was born. Once she brought in a picture of her son, and everyone agreed that Robert did look like him. Mrs. Grimsley thinks Robert is her son. She wants the impossible.

When Robert sees her come in, he shudders. He does not get along well with his own mother, so the thought of having Mrs. Grimsley as his mother irks him more. He has tried to explain to Mrs. Grimsley that he is not her son, but she won't take no for an answer. "Around the eyes," she says. "And the hair. Just like my Billy." Andrea tries to wait on Mrs. Grimsley this morning, but she will hear nothing of it. "I want Billy," she shrieks. "I want my Billy."

This particular Monday has been terrible. The 2200 broke down twice, and the repairman had to be called. It seems that every application to everything in the world is due by October 15 and everyone wants his or her copies made on 25% rag. Beverly can barely stand toward the end of the day, and all she wants to do is to go to bed with Doug. But Doug tells her he is going down to the Village to jam with some friends. Beverly is disappointed, but she doesn't say anything. "Okay, so maybe tomorrow." Doug smiles. "Maybe tomorrow." Beverly suspects Doug has another woman, but she doesn't say anything.

Steven can't take his eyes off Beverly as she tries to yank paper out of the 2200. Unlike Doug, Steven will never lose interest in her. He doesn't know what Beverly sees in Doug, but he knows Doug has lost interest in her.

Steven thinks he is becoming sterile from the photo-copying equipment. He is always careful not to get exposed to the light. Steven reads most of the information he copies, and a few months ago he copied a report from the *New England Journal of Medicine* that suggested sterility might be caused by the light in the copiers. Once every few days Steven talks about going off to a sperm bank and putting some seeds on ice. "These machines are ruining us," Steven says in the middle of a busy Monday morning. "Aren't you people concerned?"

No one is terribly concerned. Steven wouldn't be so concerned either if he didn't want to have children with Beverly. He has been in love with her since she walked into the store. He is short and Jewish, and he always falls for tall blond women who are not going to be interested in him.

As they are leaving, Steven asks Beverly if she wants to

get a bite at Bagel Nosh. It is just around the corner, and Beverly has nothing better to do, so she says, "Why not?" She wanted to go home and take a shower. Instead, she goes to Bagel Nosh. She hopes Steven will not talk about the sperm bank over dinner. She gets an onion bagel with chicken liver, and he gets a sesame bagel with lox.

Steven feels he is duty bound to level with Beverly. "Well, you know, Doug likes women, I guess. Lots of women, I mean. I'm looking for something a little more secure." Beverly knows this. Steven is the kind of man who would be looking for something more secure. Things don't come to him easily, and he isn't likely to get what he wants out of life.

As they are about to leave Bagel Nosh, Robert walks in with Andrea. They were doing the books and decided to get a bite. Andrea stares at Robert wide-eyed as if she were a fish he just caught on a line. Robert smiles brightly at Beverly, and she can tell that Andrea is jealous. Andrea thinks Robert likes Beverly. It would make sense. Everyone else does, except Doug. Beverly looks at Andrea in the Bagel Nosh reflecting glass. She is a rather dumpy brunette with frizzy hair. Andrea is the kind of woman most men would like to marry; they just don't want to date her.

Robert and Andrea sit down, and Steven is disappointed. He wanted to go to Beverly's and drink wine. He wanted to tell her about his deprived childhood in Buffalo. Steven thinks he is a marvelous storyteller and that he can charm her with his yarns. Then he wants to get her into bed. Once he is able to convince a woman to go to bed with him, she usually has no regrets. Robert and Andrea order bagels and coffee.

Robert says, "Boy, this is copy center night, huh. We just ran into Doug going uptown."

Beverly takes this in carefully as Andrea nudges Robert. "Uptown?"

Andrea says, "Oh, we didn't know which way he was going." Andrea, who helped Beverly get her job, has watched Doug go through many women at the copy center. Every time a new woman comes in, Doug, who has wonderful green eyes and thick black hair, gets interested. But then, after a month or so, he loses interest, and usually the girl has a broken heart.

Andrea has thought several times about firing Doug, but he is the fastest copier she has ever seen. Doug can keep three machines going at the same time and be hand-feeding another machine as well. Because the copy center is the busiest one in the neighborhood, Andrea can't really afford to fire him. She has tried to hint to Beverly that Doug has lost interest in her. Andrea knows the signs, because Doug lost interest in her once a few years ago.

Robert is somewhat oblivious. "No, he said he was meeting a friend at Empire Szechuan, don't you remember?"

Andrea doesn't know what else to say. "Yes, I remember."

Robert is the only one who doesn't know exactly what is going on in his store. He doesn't know, for example, that every chance she gets, Andrea tries to work beside him. He has no idea that the reason why Andrea, who once had ambitions to go to law school, has stayed at the copy center for the past three years is that she is hoping someday Robert will pay attention to her.

After a few minutes, Beverly gets up. "I'm going home." Steven gets up to go with her, but Beverly waves him down and away, as if she were the trainer of an animal act.

As Beverly climbs the stairs to her apartment, she hears the phone ringing. She counts almost fifteen rings, but she is not in a hurry to get the call. If it is not her mother, it is Doug. If it is Doug, she is not sure she wants to talk to him. When Beverly gets inside, she is glad to be alone. She is especially glad because her apartment is so quiet and the copy center is so noisy.

Beverly calls her service and tries not to be upset when she learns no one has phoned her for auditions. Like everyone in the copy center, she wants to be doing something else. In high school she was named "Most Likely to Appear on 'Saturday Night Live.' " Once a month she has new pictures of herself made up with new résumés and mails them to all the agents in New York. Andrea thinks there is no other actress in the city with that much determination. Because she is very beautiful, sometimes Beverly gets calls, but she never gets a part.

The phone rings again and Beverly answers on the fifth ring. Doug sounds anxious on the other end. "Where've you been? We finished jamming a while ago. The tenor sax never showed. Can I come up?"

Beverly wants to say no, but she says all right. She wants to say no because the truth is that she wants to be alone. She wants to read a book and wash her hair. She wants to watch "Family Feud" and call her mother. She wants to tell her mother she hasn't made it big yet and that she'd like to come home for Christmas but she can't afford it. Beverly's mother lives in a retirement village in Arizona; she always asks Beverly to visit but never sends her the money for a ticket.

There are a dozen things she wants to do, but when Doug calls, she tells him to come on up. Beverly has always had a hard time saying no to men, and she has spent too many nights with men she didn't want to be with. Doug arrives out of breath. He always runs up her steps, two steps at a time. She wonders why he does this, since he is never all that happy to see her. Beverly suspects that Doug is seeing another woman. He was probably going to see her tonight, but her husband called off his meeting, so she had to be home.

Beverly kisses Doug perfunctorily on the cheek when he

walks in. She wonders why she always falls for men who never pay much attention to her. Beverly's father died when she was fourteen, and she's never felt so betrayed before or since. She knows Doug likes to be with more than one woman at a time. He has told her he has no desire to settle down. Doug's mother has been married three times, and as far as Doug can tell, the new men were never improvements over the old ones.

After they make love, Beverly falls asleep and Doug strums his guitar. First he tunes it, then he plays "I Write the Songs That Make the Whole World Sing." In the middle of his tune, Beverly shoots out of bed. "Oh, my God!" she cries.

Doug grabs her hand. "What was it?"

"Another DC 10." Since she was a little girl, growing up near LaGuardia, Beverly's dreams have been filled with airplanes crashing into her sheets. She can be in the middle of a dream about Yosemite, a place she visited with another boyfriend she met when she did mailings for the Sierra Club, and suddenly an airplane will crash into her sheets. Beverly always wakes up when there is a crash, but otherwise she can sleep through anything.

He pulls the covers up over her chin. "You were just dreaming," he tells her. "Go back to sleep."

There are steady customers at the copy center, and Beverly knows them all. She knows Mrs. Grimsley and she knows the homosexual playwright. She knows the Jehovah's Witness, who sends prayers to his brother on Riker's Island, and the impatient woman who puts down her American Express Gold Card. She knows the music school teachers with dandruff on their collars, the desperate unemployed with their tattered résumés. And she knows a woman named Emily, who has been coming to the copy center since she began working there.

Everyone who works at the copy center is jealous of at
least one person who brings in work and stands at the other
side of the oak counter. Robert is jealous of a graphic de-
signer who does a lot of annual reports. Robert wants to
have his own graphic design business someday. Doug is
jealous of a musician who is always having his scores
printed and bound for his publisher. Steven is jealous of a
medical doctor, and Andrea is jealous of a social worker.
Beverly is jealous of Emily.

Emily comes in often. She has soft, doelike eyes, and she
cannot speak without smiling. She never comes up and says,
"I'm Ninety. Why are you taking Ninety-one?" She always says, "Excuse me. Did you call Ninety?" Beverly
knows Emily is happy and successful. Emily comes into the
copy center calmly to have the music for her newest concert run off. She has blurbs Xeroxed in which Diana Ross
says, "I'd be honored to sing any of Ms. Barkington's
songs."

Beverly doesn't suspect that Emily curses the day she had
her baby, that her work brings her no pleasure, and that
she married a record producer for his money. She has no
idea that Emily takes tranquilizers before going out, and
she has no idea that Emily is one of Doug's lovers. This
isn't some strange coincidence. Emily and Doug worked
together on a musical production in the Village two years
ago, and he's been her lover on and off ever since.

It is because of Emily that Beverly has decided to leave
the copy center, give up her acting ambitions, and go to
school in public health. Beverly bought a copy of *Are You
Really Creative?* and took the quiz in the book. Would you
rather (a) fix a clock, (b) fly a plane, (c) sit in a wild bird
sanctuary? On New Year's Eve would you rather be (a)
the life of the party, (b) the person who gives the party,
(c) the person who stays home from the party and reads a
book?

Beverly has no idea how to answer these questions, so she answers at random. Then she adds up her score and learns that "you are too ambivalent about creativity but would work well with people. Why not try a helping profession?" Since she decided to go back to school in public health, her dreams of planes have been increasing, only now she dreams of bombers, B-52s to be specific.

When Emily comes into the copy center in the afternoon, the mood is very tense. Mrs. Grimsley came in a little while ago. She wanted to make a hundred copies of a telegram from 1951 that read, "Dear Mr. and Mrs. Grimsley: We regret to inform you that your son, William, has been killed in action . . ." Mrs. Grimsley told Robert, whom she called Billy, that they were invitations to a party, and she gave a copy to him. Even Robert, who normally isn't shaken by anything, was shaken by Mrs. Grimsley.

Beverly is a little upset when Emily walks in, and she calls out her number rather impatiently. "Forty-seven," Beverly snaps, and Emily tells her she'd like to wait for Doug. Emily knows that Beverly and Doug are lovers, but Beverly has no suspicions at all. She does not even suspect when Emily hands Doug a note and Doug smiles. She thinks Doug is supposed to make a copy of the note.

That evening Doug tells Beverly he is going to jam downtown again and he'll be late, so why don't they see one another the next night. She knows he is going to meet someone else, but she has no idea it is Emily. Doug and Emily could be drug dealers, they are so discreet. Beverly is disturbed but doesn't say a word. As she is leaving the store, Steven asks if she'd like to go to dinner with him uptown. Since she has no other plans, she agrees.

They go to a burger place near West 90th and Steven orders a bacon cheeseburger. Beverly orders the same thing, because she can't make a decision. Even before their Cokes arrive, Steven grabs Beverly's hand. "Listen," he says, "Doug Cransfield isn't worth this joint on your little finger." He extracts the joint from the mass of fingers he is holding. She pulls her hand away. "It doesn't matter," she says. "I'm not looking for anything serious."

"Well, I am," Steven says boldly. "I'd like to see you more often."

"I already see you about eight hours a day." Beverly yawns and Steven frowns. "I just don't want to date much these days." She pats his hand gently. Steven and Beverly finish their burgers and walk downtown.

As they pass the 86th Street subway, they see Doug and Emily coming out of the station. There is an odd moment of recognition as Beverly thinks to herself, There's Doug with that woman. And Doug thinks he should do something, but he doesn't know what. He smiles at Beverly; there is a strange mix of guilt and affection and confusion behind his smile. Beverly thinks he looks boyish, smiling at her, with Emily holding his arm.

Doug says, "Hello," and then Beverly says, "Hello." And not knowing what else to say, Doug says, "See you tomorrow."

Because she is somewhat disoriented, Beverly does something she would not ordinarily do. She asks Steven to come over. When they get to her apartment, a place Steven has wanted to get to for a long time, he praises her choice of furniture. He praises the posters that hang over her bed. He praises the cat; he praises a rather wilting lotus plant. Finally Beverly says, "Steven, let's face it. This place is a dump."

Beverly gives the cat, named Walter, a can of 9-Lives mackerel, which he sniffs. Then he walks away. She dumps a glass of water on the plant. Then she puts on Keith Jarrett's Köln Concert and rolls a joint.

Steven is sure he will spend the night, and he hardly

knows what to do, he is so overjoyed. "I told you, baby, that guy wasn't worth your tiny toenail."

Beverly doesn't want to think about Doug at all. She gets stoned, and instead of thinking about Doug, she thinks about her father. She thinks about how she used to be afraid of the airplanes that passed so close over their house, and one day her father took her outside. He lay down in the grass and told her he was the runway and she should fly around the yard and come in for landings on his chest. So she spent the day running around their yard, making a buzzing noise, and then crashing into her father's rib cage.

Beverly is thinking about her father when Steven lunges across the candle between them and grabs her by the arm. He puts his thumbprint into her muscle. Beverly pulls back. "I'm tired," she says. She gets up, goes into her bedroom, lies down, and falls asleep.

Bewildered, Steven follows. He gets into bed with her and caresses her. Beverly wakes up screaming. "Oh, my God, two little private planes in midair!" Then she looks at Steven, unsure of what he is doing there. "Please leave," she says, and Steven, because he has almost no will where she is concerned, gets up and leaves.

The next day, when Beverly comes in to work, Doug says, "Hi," and Beverly says nothing. When Beverly is running off an actor's résumé, Doug comes over. "How are you?" He waits, but she doesn't reply. "Look, about last night . . ."

Beverly says, "There is nothing to say." And she says nothing.

She knows that Doug can stand anything but the silent treatment. His mother used to give him the silent treatment when he did something she didn't like, and it drove him crazy. Once his mother didn't talk to him for five days, and they even ate their meals together. All afternoon Doug follows Beverly around, saying dumb things like "You'd think they'd fix the fan in this place," but she doesn't respond.

Beverly knows Robert and Andrea are watching her ignore Doug, but she doesn't care. Now that she has decided to leave the copy center and go to school in public health, she can imagine herself working in a center for disease control. She knows Doug is exasperated. He stands next to her while she copies an entire book on how to grow a vegetable garden in a city apartment. "Don't be discouraged," one page reads. "You can grow fine tomato plants right in your window boxes."

Doug points to the line. "Isn't that stupid?" He laughs. "You couldn't see out the window then."

Beverly doesn't say a word. Finally Doug says, "All right, so maybe I am a jerk, but I'm trying to apologize."

She turns to him. "You are a jerk and I don't want your apology. I don't want to talk to you or see you. Just leave me alone."

When Doug walks away, Steven puts his machine on automatic. "Hey, Bev." He speaks loudly, hoping Doug will hear. "Can I see you tonight?"

She looks at Steven's small, frail body, the dark beard that hides his pockmarked face. He's not so terrible, she thinks, but she just can't stand him. "No," Beverly mumbles, "I've got plans."

Steven turns away in a huff, and later, when Beverly is leaving, he hands her an envelope. "Open this when you get home," he says to her. "It'll explain everything."

Beverly breathes a sigh of relief when she walks into her apartment. She puts a Weight Watchers veal with peppers TV dinner into the oven at 425° with the foil peeled back. She runs a bath. She calls her service and there are no messages. She gives herself a face sauna with honeysuckle facial herbs. She pours herself a glass of wine and gently eases her way into the bathtub.

Beverly often reads in the tub, so she dries her hands on a towel and opens the envelope Steven gave her as she left work. She opens it slowly, expecting to find a long letter explaining why she should not care about Doug but about him. Instead, what she finds is more to the point. What she finds is a color Xerox of a portion of the male anatomy. At the bottom he has written, "You don't know what you're missing, baby."

The next morning Beverly walks into the copy center and screams at Steven. She holds up the color Xerox so that everyone in the store can see. "What is this? Is this your idea of a joke?"

Andrea is waiting on a customer, and she turns around. Doug is making copies at two machines, and he is stunned. Steven tries to grab the page out of her hand. "Of course it's a joke. What's your problem?"

Beverly pins the Xerox to the bulletin board behind her. The place where she puts the pin makes all the men in the store wince. "This is no joke!" Beverly shouts. "You're sick. I should call the police."

Doug smiles. He has never seen Beverly so passionate, so vital. Robert is not smiling. He rips the Xerox off the board. "The customers are aware of what is going on," he says to them. "You're all fired if you don't get back to work."

"You should fire him!" Beverly shouts. "He's sick."

Steven turns off his machine. "You can't even take a joke. I'll be back later." He slides out beneath the oak counter.

Just then Mrs. Grimsley comes in, checking numbers to make certain no one has butted in front of her. Everyone in the store is upset about Beverly's fight with Steven. Robert is especially upset, because he is afraid he will lose business. When Mrs. Grimsley comes in, he decides to humor her. "How's my Billy today?" she says. She is an old woman with dark sunken eyes who probably hasn't long to live.

Robert reaches across the counter. "How'ya doing, Mom?" He pats her hand. "Boy, have I missed you."

Mrs. Grimsley looks first stunned, then angry. She pulls her hand away. "Don't you call me that. You have no right. Only my son calls me Mom." And she walks out of the store, never to return.

Beverly also walks out of the store, but she returns a few hours later. When she does, she finds a purple geranium sitting on the 2200. She hopes it is from Doug, but she knows from the handwriting it is from Steven. She opens the card and reads, "Please accept this geranium for your apartment as an apology. I am sorry if I upset you." Beverly feels bad about having shouted at him. Sometimes she thinks, working here isn't so bad.

Because she took time off in the afternoon, Beverly agrees to stay late to finish up a doctoral dissertation. Doug decides to work late with her. It is dark out as they complete their jobs at different machines. They put on the radio and listen to a program of all Sinatra. Sinatra is singing "I Did It My Way."

They turn down the bright fluorescent lights, which make them look pale green, and now the lighting is amber. Doug works on a screenplay about corruption in the police department. He reads parts of it out loud to Beverly. They agree that it sounds like all the police films they've ever seen.

Beverly is making seven copies of a dissertation on the abandonment/castration complex in men and women. As she is completing it, Doug comes up behind her. He puts his hands on her shoulders and kisses the back of her neck. He turns her to him. The green lights of the machines flash on and off. The amber lights are soothing. He takes her in his arms and pins her to the machine as he kisses her. She presses her body against Doug's and remembers what it was that made her like him in the first place. She feels the even, rhythmic pulsing of the 2200 against her spine. She prays it won't break down.

The Banana Fever

NONA does not have long to live, they say. It must be true, because she sits on the porch all day, gazing toward the jungle. Her fingers clutch the edge of the rocker or begin pointing frantically in all directions. She must see things out there. But now she is reduced to skin and bones. Her face is wrinkled and dry, and she has the faint odor of urine about her. And when I lean close to try to understand what she is muttering, her breath smells like cattle breath. Days, I sit at her side, reading to her from the newspapers that Lucinda brings once a week from the city. Though nearly mute and paralyzed, her eyes widen at certain words. Fire, revolution, execution. She must remember when she hears those words, but then she has lived almost a century here. This house, with the blue bougainvillea that stretches across the roof, has been her only empire. And her lands that extend to the edge of the jungle, to the point where the banana growers dwell.

Once a day Dr. Márquez comes and takes Nona's pulse, looks into her eyes, taps her knees. He is the one who tells me she is dying. Sometimes he says it standing beside her, and I watch her eyes widen. She is old, he says, letting his

hand fall on her silver hair. He too stares out to the place
where the banana growers dwell. Blue and red parrots
flutter back and forth through the coconut palms. Tou-
cans call and orange beaks are seen as they fly past. Lucinda brings out the lemonade and slices of meat on bread
with butter. She puts the tray down and pours lemonade
into the glass that makes a cracking sound as the cold liquid pours in.

"You waste your days, child," Lucinda says. "Tell her,
Doctor. She wastes her days sitting here beside an old
woman. Here she can learn nothing."

Though I have trouble remembering the specific events,
and though it has been so long that Nona has been con-
fined to that chair, I knew her once by the rustling of her
skirts. Always blue or yellow taffeta skirts, even in summer. She would move through the house and I always knew
where she was, and she was never far. And at night I knew
her by her deep sighs in the dark corridors of the house
when she would come to my bedside and shake her head,
wondering what to do about me. One day a messenger rode
to the house. He handed her a note, which she read and
tore into tiny pieces. She served him dinner. Then she went
upstairs and put on black, all black, and she moaned in
corners quietly to herself, and never again did her skirts
rustle or did she come and stand at my bedside at night,
shaking her head. And she never spoke Jorge's name and
he never came home that Easter, so that was how Lucinda
and I knew he had been killed. But Nona never said.

It is siesta time now and the doctor has left. He always
comes just in time for some lunch and leaves for his siesta.
The village is quiet; all the shades are drawn. We live in
this house without men, and all of the women, even Margarita, sleep alone in their beds. Sometimes they return.
They come down at night and sit around the kitchen table. Once a year or every two years. I am allowed only to

look at them and then I must go to bed. They are like the cowboys I have seen in the Westerns that play sometimes in the town nearby. Lucinda says it is a sin, what has been happening. It is siesta time now and I sit on the porch beside Nona. Everywhere there is the scent of bananas. When I sleep, I can smell the bananas, and when I have nightmares, they are filled with the tarantulas that hide in the bunches. Santiago has a scar on his back where a tarantula on the banana plantation bit him and the foreman took a knife and dug into the flesh to remove the venom. I have seen tarantulas walk out from under the porch when the sun goes down. Nona sits on the porch, under the awning. The town is white in the glow of the porch, and everything is a brilliant white, as if on fire, and there is the scent of bananas. But during siesta time we no longer hear the sound of chopping.

The Indians are everywhere. They speak Quechua and Aymara and they have come down from the Andes. They have taught me to speak their languages. They tell me stories about how creatures from another planet named Lake Titicaca, "the jaguar pounces." About the chain of gold that reached from the Island of the Sun to the Island of the Moon and was severed and dropped into the sea, never to be found, when the Spaniards arrived. They tell me of Atahuelpa, who offered a room filled with gold in exchange for his life, and when his men produced the gold, filling the great hall, the Spaniards tied him to four horses and sent them running in four different directions. Since then, the Indians say, they have been docile in the face of the conquerors. They perform their chores and work steadily all day long at the banana plantation, but underneath I know they are restless. They are tired of being servants. I have attended their ceremonies where they ask the sun to bring back the old ways. They have these ceremonies deep in the jungle at the sites of old cities. The cities

are in ruin, overgrown with moss and thick lianas. Someday this town we live in will be just as overgrown. Already it is in a state of decay. When I used to ask Nona
about my parents, she would shake her head and sigh. Poor
child, she used to say. When I asked the Indians at one of
their ceremonies, they told me that my parents were a
swamp and I was born of their mud the way all frogs and
natural creatures are born. That is how I know that I am
illegitimate, because they have invented a myth for my
benefit.

I have often wondered why I am here. Why I was left
behind when the others went. "Because Nona needed you,"
Lucinda said. Lucinda remembers almost everything that
ever happened around here. She is almost as old as Nona
and a Quechua. "Long ago," Lucinda says as we sit on
the porch in the shade, "some men came to this part of
the forest. They brought machetes and guns. They drew
lines on the ground with their machetes and made borders. The next thing we knew there was a road that seemed
to go nowhere, but on that road machines came; they puffed
and the Indians all believed that it was the end of the world
because monsters had returned. And then they planted. It
has never been the same since." And when I ask her what
it was like before, her eyes grow dim. "It was quiet," she
says, "always quiet, like at siesta time, and the men were
home."

Miguel arrives in the afternoon. No one knows where he
came from or how long he will stay but only that he has
come home for a while. Margarita rushes downstairs and
embraces him. Tears fill her eyes. "It won't be long," he
says to her.

He kisses everyone hello. He looks at Nona. "I don't remember her being so bad," he says. He holds her face in
his hands, but she does not seem to recognize him. I stand

in the doorway, watching him move slowly from room to room. He closes the shades. He looks around. He has grown suspicious, it seems. He asks if they have been here to inquire after him. We shake our heads. They stopped coming long ago, we tell him. They used to come once, twice, a week, but we did not know anything and if we had, we would not have told them. Miguel travels through the house like a hunted dog. He is careful; he stays close to the corners and keeps his eyes on the exits. He is larger than I remember him. I remember him being shorter and plump, but now he smells of sweat and his body is covered with hair. He has grown dark and sullen. He is only seven years older than I, but he seems as old as Nona and Lucinda. It was two years ago that he rode off. Messages came from time to time. Perhaps more were sent, but they were intercepted. The messages were always short and they never told us where he was or when he would return. Once a messenger rode to the house on horseback and told us that Miguel was dead, and Margarita cried the entire day until the next day, when we found out from the priest it was not true. It had been a trick for us to lead them to him.

"So, little cousin," he says, "you've grown up, I see." I blush and move back into a corner of the room. Margarita stares at me. It seems as if it is the first time she has ever looked at me. At lunch we all sit down together at the table. Nona sits at the head and Lucinda feeds her. Food drips onto her chin. She does not speak; she only stares. Since her last stroke, she gives no sign of knowing any of us, except for the slight dilation of her eyes that comes from time to time. Miguel sits across from me. Absently, Margarita runs her fingers over his arm.

"So," Lucinda says, "when will you marry?" Margarita lowers her eyes. Everyone knows that Lucinda is often thoughtless about the questions she asks.

"When this is finished," Miguel replies. His answer to

that question has always been the same. Always, when this is finished. It is four years now that Margarita has waited. She never seems to tire of waiting. It suits her, delays, hesitations, virtuous waits. Margarita lives for the day when Miguel will marry her the way she lives for the hereafter. It is the certainty of the coming of both that allows her to enjoy the waiting. Nona stares at Miguel and I believe she must see him now. Her eyes roll nervously in their sockets and she smiles a thin smile. "Grandma," Miguel says, observing her changed expression. "Does she know me, Lucinda?"

Lucinda shrugs her shoulders. She hopes that Nona does not recognize this man, who for her is a bandit, who eats at her table with his gun and holster strapped to his waist, bullets crisscrossed on his chest. His skin is hardened from the sun and the rain and he looks older than all of us. Around his neck, he wears a small charm that I have not seen before and that Margarita begins to touch. She fondles the charm and I can see that it is a gold banana.

"What's this," she asks, tugging on it. She has never seen the charm before, and because I know Margarita, I know that she is worried that another woman gave it to him. Miguel brushes her hand away. He reaches for the lamb shank on his plate and picks it up. He bites down and slowly chews the meat. "What is it," Margarita repeats and Miguel tucks the charm into his shirt.

"It's to keep the banana fever away," he says.

Margarita is afraid because she has heard about the killer bees and she has heard that they are moving north. Two hundred miles south, they killed a man and two cattle. One hundred miles south, they killed a horse and a child. They are aggressive and they attack whatever moves. They attack in a swarm, and five stings can kill a man. On the porch, Margarita sits beside Nona while Miguel sleeps upstairs. He has been sleeping since he finished lunch on the previous day. We all agree that we have never seen anyone sleep so hard or so long. While she sits on the porch, her eyes scan the hills, searching for the killer bees that she has not stopped talking about since Lucinda heard new reports in the town this morning. I know that in her mind she sees the swarms coming out of the hill, attacking her, Nona, Miguel. While Nona rocks, Margarita tells her about the bees and where they are coming from and what they can do.

All the time she talks, she does her lace work. She has been working on the lace for her wedding veil for three years. The dress she completed two years ago. It took her four years. When the dress and veil are completed, she says, she will marry Miguel. Even if it is not yet time according to him. Sometimes when I watch her, with her pitch-black hair and pale skin, she looks as if she were making her shroud. It has taken so long. First there was the weaving, the blocking, the cutting. It is as if when she completes this gown and its veil, she will die. The material is so white and clean and she has been working on it for years now, so I believe she will be buried in it. She will die as she came into this world. As pure and white as the dress she has worked on steadily these past six years. The dress is so white and Margarita so pale that they all seem to blend into the town, which during siesta time is white as if on fire.

She works slowly today and I can tell that she is anxious because Miguel is home and because Lucinda has told her more stories about the killer bees. As she works on the veil, she pierces her thumb with the needle. Blood oozes from the thumb and a droplet touches the lace. Margarita screams. She screams not because the lace is spoiled — she knows it will wash right out — but because it is a bad omen. She dips it in a glass of cold water at her side and it leaves no stain, but still she cries. "I will have to make another one," she says, wiping her tears with her handkerchief. "Look, Nona, I have to make another. This one will bring us bad luck." And then she begins to cry again because of the blood and because of Miguel and because Nona, they say, is finally dying. She cries because she has pricked her finger and she is afraid she will never marry. But mostly she cries because the heat of siesta time stings her flesh like thorns.

Margarita stands with her ear pressed to the door, listening. "If he goes," she mutters, "if he goes this time . . ." Her voice trails off, filled with her sadness. If he goes, what. Won't she wait as she always has? Margarita's waiting is like Nona's being alive: something that seems to be a fact of life, something that will always be here, like the coconut palms and the blue bougainvillea. Santiago leaves the kitchen and we are able to look inside. They are seated in a circle. The room is dark and they have set up a shortwave. Impulses come through the short-wave, a steady beeping sound from somewhere in the jungle. They are out there, I hear them whispering. I hear the beeps and Antonio is writing them down, deciphering the code.

Lucinda comes to the doorway, looking for Santiago. "He went outside for air," Antonio says. Lucinda nods and puts her hands on my shoulders. In Quechua, I ask her what they are discussing and what is going to happen, and she puts her fingers to her lips to shush me. I ask her why I have to be so quiet, why everyone talks in whispers tonight, and she shushes me again. Margarita leans against the doorway, waiting for Miguel to give her his decision. In the drawing room, Nona sits. Her lips move back and forth, as if she were reciting her rosary. She mutters to herself and the words are nonsense, like the code the men receive. Sometimes, though, I hear her say Jorge, and I know she is seeing him as he rode through town on that white horse, celebrating a premature victory.

Santiago returns and Lucinda stops him in the doorway. Two months ago he found his dog and his son with their heads severed by a machete. They had been trespassing on the land of the banana growers. Since then, he has hated them as much as Miguel. Tarantulas, he calls them. Many-legged creatures filled with poison. Lucinda stands between Santiago and the kitchen. He is her only living relative, her grandson. "Will you go if they go?" Santiago shrugs his shoulders. Lucinda asks again and he nods. Lucinda steps back and Santiago returns to the kitchen.

I have never seen the banana growers because I am not allowed to go into that part of the jungle. I just know that they are out there, the way I know snakes and wildcats are out there. Margarita taps me on the shoulder and points upstairs. The men sit, bullets strapped around their chests, listening to the beeps. The room is dark and hazy with their smoke. I kiss Nona and slowly climb the stairs.

I pull back the mosquito netting over my bed, and the netting is moist with humidity. The moonlight shines on the wooden floor and the netting appears luminous. The air smells heavy but fresh with nectar, because now is the time when the flowers are in bloom. I have to fight to keep the bougainvillea from coming into my room. Downstairs Nona sits and I know she will outlive us all. As I drift to sleep, I hear voices and my dreams seem to be messages sent over the miles, messages in a code that I cannot decipher, as if someone wanted to tell me something very important but could not make me understand. Later I wake. It is still dark and from somewhere in the house I hear the sound of crying.

In the morning Margarita is gone. To the city, Miguel tells me, where it is safer. For some reason I believe that he is lying. I go into her room but it is empty. On the dresser is her veil. The room seems sadly expectant, the way Margarita always seemed to me. Nona is already down on the porch, where Lucinda has carried her. She is tiny now; she cannot weigh more than a hundred pounds. I never see her eat. Only drink the thick liquids Lucinda prepares. Miguel paces the house all day. He walks from room to room. He paces and then he sits and then he rises and begins pacing again. He watches. Miguel was always a watcher. He watches the jungle for some sign. He watches me as I move through the kitchen while he eats alone.

"I heard crying," I say as he eats.

"She did not want to leave," he says, "but it will be better. Her people are there. Here she will rot."

I go to Nona on the porch and ask her why Margarita went away. Nona stares at me and her eyes widen as I mention Margarita's name. "An unpredictable girl," Lucinda says. "You never knew when she'd flare up." All day long I sit and watch the jungle. The air is heavy and smells like rotting wood and stagnating water. Miguel sits in the kitchen as it grows darker, jotting down notes and listening to the short-wave. He shakes his head back and forth as the messages come through.

That night after dinner I go to bed early. I sit up reading by a small lantern. Miguel comes into my room. "Little cousin," he says. He lifts the mosquito netting and takes the book from my hand. He touches my cheek and turns down the light of the lantern. He removes the charm from around his neck. "If you are ever in danger, send this with a messenger you trust. All he has to do is show it to the people he encounters along the way, and they will lead him to me. When I see this, I will come. No matter where I am." He places the charm around my neck. "It is your safety." Then he pulls back the covers and looks at me for a long time with his steady green eyes. He runs his fingers through my hair. Then he lies down beside me and moves his hand on my belly.

The news over the radio is not good. Lucinda and Nona and I sit by the radio and listen and it is not good. In the distance we still hear the sound of chopping, the sound of the banana workers at work. We listen, and Nona rocks back and forth. I put my hand on my belly, on the spot where Miguel placed his the night before. I can still feel the pressure of his hand there. With my other hand, I absently hold on to the charm.

"Where did you get that?" Lucinda asks, trying to tug it from around my neck. I pull away. "Did he put that on you?" She orders me to take it off, but I refuse. "Poor child," she says in Quechua. "You are marked as if you had been branded. They should have taken you from this place years ago."

I go with Chalo, the dog, for a walk around the perimeter of the town. He leaps into the air and darts ahead of me, barking. He is nervous about something. No one is outside. The streets are white in the rays of the sun and the town is dusty. It is quiet, it is suddenly so quiet. I wonder if this was the way it was quiet before the machines came, the way Lucinda said. But it is too quiet. Even the monkeys and parrots are still. Then I hear a noise, a very loud noise, and I think of Nona. This time it seems that she really is dying. I run back to the house, with Chalo rushing at my side, barking all the way, and on the porch I see Nona alone. Her eyes are wider than ever before, wide as if she had just been stabbed somewhere. And her lips are moving swiftly and she mutters the same sound over and over again. I lean forward and press my ear to her lips. Her lips are moist and the air she breathes into my ear is very hot. "Bees," she says. "Bees." I look out toward the jungle. The air seems heavy with sweetness; the town is hot. It emits a yellow glow, a sickly pale yellow glow. Again there comes the strong scent of bananas, but it is not siesta time and there is no sound of chopping. I look out to the hills and I see the swarm where Nona is pointing. She continues pointing and stammering the first word she has uttered that I have understood in a long time, but she is mistaken. They are small, so I can see how she made her error; tiny like insects. "No, Nona," I say, trying to restrain her. "No," I repeat, helping her sit back down, "it's only men."

Death Apples

FOR REASONS that would never be clear to her, Rita Hoffman invited her mother to a Caribbean island to recover. Mrs. Hoffman had a lot to recover from. The divorce from her second husband being one. The death of her first husband being another. The death of her parents, of her firstborn in a car crash. In sum, Rita invited her mother to recover from her life.

Rita thought the island would be a perfect place. But there was nothing to do that Mrs. Hoffman liked to do. There was no shopping, no good restaurants, and not many white people. There were things about the island that Rita liked, though. She liked the lizards who blew up their red porous pouches and humped up and down when they seemed to be listening. She liked the little furry mongooses that slunk across the roads, bellies to the ground, and she liked to look at the bodies of the West Indian men. She liked swimming among the barracuda of Ginger Bay. And she liked the warning signs painted on the manchineel trees. Killer trees. Trees that if you touched them would take your life away. Rita liked all the things she discovered during their first three days while her mother slept.

Shortly after they arrived at the tiny island a few hundred miles east of Puerto Rico, Mrs. Hoffman said, "Honey, your mother needs her beauty rest," and she went to bed. Rita didn't know what to make of it. Her mother got up at noon, walked out to the patio, went back to bed, and slept until cocktails. Then she made it through dinner and went to bed again. Rita figured her mother was just tired, but by the third day this period of rest seemed to be getting a little long. It occurred to Rita that perhaps her mother had come here to die.

So the next day Rita rented a moped for her mother. "Mom," she said, waking her with a tray of coffee and rolls and fresh-squeezed orange juice, "it's time you tested your wings."

"My wings seem a bit weary," her mother replied. But then she said, "You're right. I suppose I should venture forth." Mrs. Hoffman got out of bed. She opened her striped cotton hospital robe, the only thing she'd kept — except for his name — that had belonged to Rita's father, whom she had nursed for the last six months of his life. At night, while her father lay upstairs, dying, Rita would go downstairs and in the darkened living room see just one red light, from a cigarette, glowing in the dark. Her mother would say, "Honey, is that you?" and Rita would sneak back up the stairs.

Mrs. Hoffman let the robe slip off her shoulders and onto the ground. Rita saw her mother, standing there, naked. Her thighs and hips were turning to flab; her breasts sagged. In her legs, thick blue veins like rivers twisted and ran. She had borne three children, and the oldest, James, had died in a car crash, speeding on an L.A. freeway, though the police said he wouldn't have had a scratch on him if he'd been wearing his seat belt. James had always been reckless, like their mother. Rita had her mother's body, she knew that, and now she could see what she'd look like in twenty-five years. Everything in Rita's life had thus far been directed toward one simple goal, the only real goal in Rita's life. She was determined not to grow up to be like her mother.

Mrs. Hoffman had never been on a moped before, but she was willing to try anything once. On their way to the moped place, Mrs. Hoffman glanced into all the windows of shops. She looked at the rose-colored shells and the T-shirts that read I'VE DONE IT AT THE BOTTOM OF THE SEA. She wore dark glasses with pale blue rims that winged up at the sides, and she lifted them from time to time, staring at her own reflection in the glass. "I don't look so bad, do I? For an old dame?"

Rita looked at her mother in the Bermuda shorts that didn't quite fit, the polo shirt that clung too tightly to her breasts. "You look terrific, Mom."

Mrs. Hoffman tucked her arm through her daughter's. "I needed to get away." As they walked, her mother looked at her reflection again. A group of Caribbean men on their way to the sugar cane fields watched them as they walked past. The men had dark skin and arms with thick working muscles. Their bellies were taut. They were accustomed to the white women who came down from the north. Sometimes they made love to them. Sometimes they married them. Rita looked at the men as they passed, and Rita supposed that the men had no right to look at her in that way. Rita supposed incorrectly. The men were not looking at her in that way. They were looking mostly at Rita's mother.

Just before they reached the moped place, her mother paused. "How could it have slipped my mind? I forgot to tell you. Did you hear about Russ Stapleton?" Rita couldn't help being stunned. Her mother hadn't mentioned Russ to her in ten years, perhaps more. Not since her father died.

But Rita was certain, if she thought about it, that she hadn't spent a single day without thinking about him. And if Rita thought about it further, she knew there was no reason that her mother should even mention Russ Stapleton to her, yet her mother had said it in such a way that Rita had to assume her mother knew something about Rita that Rita didn't know her mother knew.

"He's getting divorced."

"Oh," Rita said. They had reached the moped place. Charlie, the huge fair-skinned man with fifteen tattoos — Rita had counted fifteen, up and down his arms — greeted them. He pointed to the moped Rita's mother was supposed to ride. Rita turned to her mother. "Is he really getting divorced? That's incredible."

"Oh." Her mother nodded. "That doesn't surprise me so much. I was more surprised when he didn't marry you."

Mrs. Hoffman took to the moped right away, after a brief lesson from Charlie. He sent them off on the ocean road, heading toward the ruins of Gustavberg, the old sugar cane plantation at the tip of the island. Rita checked to make sure her mother could drive the thing up the hill and use her brakes and not sail over the handlebars. And when Rita was sure of that, she took off.

Rita liked to fly. She liked to ride horses and bikes and motorcycles. She liked fast-moving trains and low-flying planes. When she'd been younger, she'd been reckless, like James. She'd liked riding on Russ Stapleton's Harley when he used to pick her up at night in the canyon and take her down to the sea.

It wasn't Russ who gave Rita her first kiss. It was some other boy, now faded into the memory of so many other nondescript boys who'd kissed her during spin the bottle or after movie dates. But it didn't matter who the others were or how old or when it happened, because for Rita there was only one night that mattered.

It was the night when Russ came over and said he wanted to talk, so they'd gone down to the ocean. But when they got there, he didn't seem to have anything to say. They'd been friends since they were children, and Leslie, Russ's girlfriend, was a good friend of Rita's. Rita asked him if anything was wrong with Leslie, and Russ had shaken his head. He'd taken her by the hand and walked in silence, the Pacific roaring at their feet. Then, suddenly, without a word, there on the beach with the warm breeze blowing off the ocean, he'd kissed her. She felt as if there were no world beyond the world of his lips on her lips. Nothing had prepared her for this. Nothing would ever be like it again. That kiss had wakened Rita as if she'd been sleeping her entire life.

She shuddered as the moped zipped along the ocean road. Rita had spent most of her life falling in or out of love with the wrong men. And not a single one of them had ever done for her what Russ did when he kissed her that night on the beach. And not a single one had ever done to her what Russ did when he married Leslie.

Black men grinned at Rita and her mother as they took the curves on their mopeds. Mrs. Hoffman waved and laughed. Defiantly she passed Rita. Most of the black people of the island were descendants of the slaves who had worked that plantation, and the sugar cane industry had declined since the slaves were freed. Mrs. Hoffman and Rita zipped along, waving at descendants of slaves, until they came near the ruins of the sugar cane plantation.

At the plantation they parked their mopeds and walked. They walked past beautiful trees named flamboyant, the frangipani, the genip, the sugar pear. And the manchineel. When they got to the manchineel, Mrs. Hoffman stopped. She stopped at the big red spot on the trees and the sign beneath them, the warning. These trees are fatal, the sign said. You cannot eat their fruit. On the trees Mrs. Hoffman and Rita saw little reddish-yellow apples, like crabapples, and another sign told them that these were called death apples. That Columbus, the great discoverer of America, had named them death apples because his men, thinking they were in paradise, had eaten of them and died.

That evening for dinner they went to a beach bar and ordered piña coladas and sea turtle steaks. Mrs. Hoffman talked about the breakup of her second marriage. She told Rita how she almost died of boredom with Ben. "Golf and gin rummy; that's all he ever talked about. In all of L.A., he'd only eat in three restaurants, and two of them were his private clubs." Rita laughed and her mother ordered another piña colada and a bottle of white wine. "But, you know, even when you want out," Mrs. Hoffman said, "it's always difficult to break up with somebody. Ben used to fix all the appliances in the house. He'd fix the dishwasher, the dryer, whatever. Do you know what I did when he left me? I showed up one day at his office with the toaster."

As Mrs. Hoffman poured Rita a glass of wine, they both laughed at the thought of Mrs. Hoffman arriving at Ben's office with a broken toaster. Mrs. Hoffman patted her daughter's hand. "I want you to marry a good man. Are you seeing anybody now?"

Rita had been seeing somebody for the past three years, but she didn't want to tell her mother about him. He was the lawyer she worked for as a paralegal. After hours, they made love on the red vinyl sofa in his office. He was supposed to leave his wife, and sometimes he got closer to it than other times. "What about Russ?" Mrs. Hoffman asked. "Maybe you should call him. After a while, of course."

Rita turned her wine glass in her hands. "Mom, I didn't know you knew anything about it."

"You'd be surprised what I know," Mrs. Hoffman said. Then she added softly, "I'm your mother."

"Anyway, it was over ten years ago."

"Go for it," Mrs. Hoffman said, "while you still can."

Just then a group of boys, young men really, came into the beach bar. They wore Bermuda shorts and T-shirts and were drinking beer out of bottles. Rita counted thirteen of them. They formed a line and said they were called the Baker's Dozen from Yale University and they were going to sing. First they sang, "There ain't nobody here but us chickens." They tucked their thumbs into their armpits and clucked like chickens. And then they sang "Mammy" in a good Al Jolson rendition.

Rita and her mother were laughing and enjoying themselves. Then, for the next number, a young man with a head of auburn curls and blue eyes stepped forward. The beach bar was filling up, with tourists milling around. The young man glanced around.

Rita noticed her mother looking intensely at the young man, and the young man suddenly fixed his eyes on Rita's mother. He stared at her with a deep look of longing as he began to sing, in a beautiful tenor voice, "Oh, ye take the high road and I'll take the low road, and I'll be in Scotland afore ye." Rita put down her fork and her glass of wine. Her mother stared deep into the eyes of the young man, and the young man stared at her. "But me and my true love will never meet again, on the bonnie, bonnie banks of Loch Lomond."

After he finished singing, he stepped back into the crowd and disappeared. But Mrs. Hoffman continued to stare at the place where he'd been. "Your father," she mumbled, rubbing her eyes, "he used to sing to me like that when he was that boy's age."

Rita motioned for the waiter to get them their check. Mrs. Hoffman continued to scan the restaurant, searching for the boy who'd sung "Loch Lomond." When she was convinced that the boy had left, she shook her head as if waking up. Then she caught Rita by the hand. "Listen," she

said, "I'm going to tell you something. I don't know if you
want to hear this, but I'm going to tell you. I loved your
father more than I've ever loved anything. More than I
loved you and your brothers."

Rita didn't think she wanted to hear more. She was eager to leave. "You don't have to tell me any of this, Mom."
She knew her mother was drunk, and she wanted to get
out of the restaurant before they embarrassed themselves.

But her mother went on. "If there's a kind of love that
kills, I've had it. It eats away. It wants too much. That's
not good love." Rita started to get up, but her mother
pulled her down. "When he died, I buried myself. I dug a
deep hole and I went in. And now this is what's left and
I'm going to make the most of it." And she clasped her
daughter by the wrist.

Rita paid the bill and helped her mother up. She lifted her
mother and took her by the arm. Rita's mother leaned on
Rita as she led her slowly along the beach, back to their
room. In their room Rita undressed her mother. She took
off her blouse and her skirt. She helped her mother into a
nightgown. Her mother pulled her knees to her chest, the
way she always slept, and curled into a fetal position. Then
Rita kissed her mother as Mrs. Hoffman drifted to sleep.

Rita lay in her bed by the window with the view of the
sea and the full moon. Mrs. Hoffman began to snore. Often
Rita had to poke or kick her mother in the middle of the
night to keep her from snoring so loud. Rita had shared
rooms with her mother before. When her mother was
married to Ben, and Rita would come to visit, Ben always
went to sleep on the sofa bed and Rita slept with her
mother.

Rita never liked Ben. He was a cardboard box entrepre-
neur. When he was courting Rita's mother, he came over
one afternoon with a sample of each of his cardboard boxes.

He made Rita, who was already in her late teens, crawl under one of the boxes and he'd crawl under another. He wanted to surprise Mrs. Hoffman when she came home from work. Rita never knew what her mother saw in anyone but her father.

When her father was dying, Rita's mother often got in bed with her. Rita remembered how her mother would wrap her arms tightly around Rita's shoulders and curl herself up against Rita's back and how Rita would want to push her away, not feel her breasts pointed against her back, not smell her stale, cigarette breath. And sometimes as her father lay dying in the next room, Rita could hear him calling her mother, and her mother in her sleep would clasp Rita tighter, not wanting to hear or let go of Rita. Rita felt like the log a drowning person clings to.

Rita knew now that her mother had probably heard her father calling in the night and that her mother had clung to Rita while she pretended not to hear. Rita knew now that her mother had come into Rita's bed not because she felt alone and wanted Rita's company. She had come because she was weaning Rita's father of this world.

In the morning they got on their mopeds and went to Ginger Bay. Rita asked her mother if she wanted to go snorkeling and her mother said no. She said, "I've lived all these years without putting my face in water except to wash it, so why should I put it in now."

"I thought you'd try anything once, Mom."

Her mother nodded. "Except get more wrinkles," she said as she rubbed Coppertone #4 all over her face and put on a sun visor. Then Mrs. Hoffman stretched out on their blankets. "Besides, what's to see at the bottom of the sea?" She laughed and pointed in the direction of some West Indian men on the beach. "I've got plenty to look at right here."

Rita got into the water and put on her fins, her snorkel, her mask. She saw her mother, propped up on her elbows, scanning the beach. Rita swam. She followed the signs put up by the Department of the Interior. This is coral. This is fire coral; do not touch. This is healthy coral. This is unhealthy coral. Dying coral. Dead coral. This Is Destruction: Coral being destroyed by boring organisms.

As Rita swam, she thought about Russ and what it would be like when she talked to him. What she would say. She wondered if it would be possible to go back again, and she thought it probably would not. When Rita finished her swim, she walked, stumbling in her flippers, back to where her mother lay. She plopped down beside her. "You should go in. It's beautiful."

"I like the land," her mother said.

"There're these funny signs in the water," Rita said, thinking about the little signs put there by the Department of the Interior. "One says, 'Coral being destroyed by boring organisms.' "

Mrs. Hoffman laughed. "Just like my second marriage." She flipped over. "Honey, put some cream on my back, will you?"

"You think you'll ever marry again, Mom?" Rita asked, wiping her hands and face with the towel.

"Naw." Her mother sighed. "Who'd have me now?"

Rita took the Coppertone and squirted it on her hand. She hesitated at her mother's back. She didn't want to feel the texture of sand and cream and her mother's skin, but she took a deep breath and rubbed.

In the evening they went to a fish fry in the town, and later Mrs. Hoffman wanted to go dancing. She wanted Rita to take her to the reggae bar near the harbor, and Rita said, Why not? In the bar the moon hung over the yachts in the harbor, and white women drank rum. The band set up and slowly began to play their drums. Mrs. Hoffman kept the beat with her hand on the bar. Then she began to tap her feet, and her body started to sway.

Her mother looked old to Rita. Her blond hair was bleached and her wrinkles more pronounced because of the afternoon at Ginger Bay. Her nail polish was chipping. Mrs. Hoffman looked like a secretary who doesn't bother with her appearance any longer.

Her mother wanted to dance. She turned to Rita and said, "I'm going to dance." Rita told her mother she should do whatever made her happy.

Black men were clustered in the corners. Since the native women didn't go to the reggae bars, several men danced by themselves. Rita's mother swayed and twisted at the bar almost, but not quite, in time to the music. It wasn't long before someone asked her to dance. Her mother winked at Rita, and Rita winked back. The man put his hand on Mrs. Hoffman's hip, and Mrs. Hoffman started to move. The man put his hand more firmly on Mrs. Hoffman's hip and began guiding her along the dance floor.

Rita watched her mother. Her mother didn't have the beat yet, but she tossed her head back and laughed, and so did the West Indian man. Then another man cut in and the first man disappeared. The second man who danced with Rita's mother was taller and more assured. The first man came to the bar and asked Rita to dance, but Rita said no.

Mrs. Hoffman motioned for Rita to join her, but Rita shook her head and smiled. The first man who danced with Rita's mother was insistent, and finally Rita agreed to dance with him. He pulled Rita close and sang into her ear, "I am the conqueror. I am the master of my race." He sang very loud. It was the song the band was singing, but the words had a harshness inside Rita's ear.

Rita looked at her mother. She waved her hands and

rocked. The woman who'd slept for three days was suddenly a bundle of energy. Rita saw her mother's flesh shining through her slacks. She saw the line of her mother's underpants, visible through Mrs. Hoffman's white slacks. She watched the flab of her mother's thighs, her breasts, as her mother danced. She watched the fat that hung from her arms as her mother moved. "Your sister is a good dancer," said the man who danced with Rita.

Rita was shocked. "That's my mother," she said.

But the man opened his mouth wide and laughed, his white teeth shimmering. "That's no mother," he replied.

Suddenly Mrs. Hoffman was surrounded by men who wanted to dance with her. Sweat poured from her brow; her polo shirt clung to her breasts. Her slacks were damp with wet spots that clung to her flesh. Her smile grew coy and girlish. Her laughter was carefree. What if she goes home with one of them, Rita thought.

The music picked up, and Rita wanted to leave, but she couldn't. She tried to follow the man dancing with her, but her eyes were now suddenly fixed on her mother. She couldn't stop staring. Rita watched her mother, sweating, hair stuck to her skull, nipples erect under her polo shirt, white slacks clinging to her thighs, dancing for her life.

The next morning Rita wouldn't get out of bed. Her mother tried to wake her three or four times, but Rita just told her mother to leave her alone. Then Mrs. Hoffman went down to the beach bar without her. She ordered bacon and eggs, grits and coffee, juice, and she brought a tray back to Rita. "You had too much rum," her mother said.

Rita wanted to be left alone, but her mother made her sit up and eat. "Darling," Mrs. Hoffman said, running her hand over her daughter's brow. Rita pulled away. "Don't be angry about last night. I just wanted to dance."

"Leave me alone. Why won't you let me sleep?" Rita groaned. This vacation had been a terrible idea. She didn't know what had made her think of it in the first place. But in a few days they'd be home, and she'd never again plan another trip like this.

"Come on," her mother said, handing her two Bufferins. "Let's get out. I want to go to Ginger Bay."

They decided to take the long way, past the sugar cane plantation. They followed the coast road, overlooking the turquoise sea, little islands dotting it. Watermelon Island, Fat Virgin Island, Smuggler's Island, Pirate's Cove. They rode fast, Mrs. Hoffman ahead most of the time, and then they came to the manchineel trees again. And as she'd done the time before, Mrs. Hoffman stopped. She stared at the trees, their branches laden with death apples.

Then she reached her hand into the sky and plucked one from the tree. She plucked it and held it up as if she'd just caught it out of the sky. Then she pretended to take a bite. Rita waited for her mother's hand to burn. Mrs. Hoffman held the death apple in her hand and pretended to take another bite. "Honey," her mother said, "you've got no idea. I've had the time of my life."

Rita kicked the kick stand on her bike and walked over to her mother. Age lines were deep on her face. The sun made her skin look dry, her hair frizzy. Mrs. Hoffman stared at her own reflection in Rita's glasses. "You are my daughter," Mrs. Hoffman said, offering her the apple. Rita took the apple from her mother's hand and wrapped her arm around her mother. "You are my beautiful, beautiful daughter," Mrs. Hoffman said, "and I never taught you how to live."

When they reached Ginger Bay, Mrs. Hoffman's hand was turning red and so was Rita's, only less so. "I can't believe it," Mrs. Hoffman said. "Columbus was right." Rita looked at her mother's hand and told her it was a dumb thing to do, but that she thought a little salt water would do them both good.

"Yes," Mrs. Hoffman said, "I thought I'd try snorkeling today. Why don't you show me what to do, dear?" So Rita put on her own gear and showed her mother how to put on her snorkel, her mask, her flippers. Rita showed her mother how to breathe through the tube. Rita watched as her mother's eyes darted inside her mask, looking to Rita for guidance. The distortion of the mask hid the harshness of Rita's mother's face. The lines around the eyes softened. The face assumed the gentleness of the water around them. Her eyes blended in with the green sea. Years seemed to drift away or mean nothing.

Rita stuffed the snorkel into her mother's mouth. "Now breathe, Mom. Like this. Through your mouth." Rita breathed and her mother watched. Then her mother breathed and Rita watched. At first her breath sputtered forth. Rita laughed and so did her mother. Then her mother breathed a deeper breath.

They thrust their faces into the water, and Mrs. Hoffman looked to Rita for directions, her eyes wide, expectant. They pushed off into the warm, resilient water. Her mother followed in Rita's wake. Rita felt her mother at the back of her flippers as she moved toward the reefs. Mrs. Hoffman had been a housewife all her life and had never seen the bottom of the sea.

They followed the trail the Department of the Interior had marked with little blue signs. They saw angelfish and black fish with iridescent blue spots and bright yellow tails. They swam along the reef where parrot fish and small barracuda fed.

When they completed the trail, her mother said she wanted to find another reef, but this time she wanted to go where there were no signs. Rita had found one across the bay while her mother slept, so she knew which way to go. They moved in unison. They moved like twins on their way, preparing to greet the light of the new world.

Links

A T MY GRANDMOTHER'S FUNERAL, an old boy-friend of mine showed up. He saw the obituary in the paper and was certain I'd be in town. The year before she died, my grandmother had me meet her in Miami, and we had a wonderful time in a rented car, cruising up and down the main drag. Whenever I met her in Miami, we always went to the pet shop, owned by a reclusive cousin who hated company, and my grandmother always made the cousin open all the cages so that she could play with the animals. Many years earlier she'd taken me to see the great ape Bushman in a Chicago zoo. Before I was born, Bushman, in a fit of loneliness, embraced his keeper, crushing him in his arms. No one ever entered his cage again; my grandmother said that was no way to live. Her funeral was held on an Indian summer afternoon, one of those hot, in-explicable days that sometimes come after the first frost, just before winter sets in. The sugar maples dropped leaves like gold nuggets on the family plot. The plot has room for all my great-aunts and uncles and for my parents but not for me. I am expected to marry and be buried some-where else with my husband's family.

I don't remember a thing about the funeral, except the transplanted rabbi, with his Brooklynese, who kept saying "bee-u-tea-ful," referring to my grandmother. She died in her nineties, the matriarch, and family squabbles never reached her ears; she died without knowing that my mother and one of her brothers hadn't spoken, except in her presence, in ten years. When the first shovelfuls of dirt were dropped, I turned away. That was when I saw George. He was standing in the outer circle with friends, not family, and he was dressed in black, which I wasn't, and his eyes seemed to have a real sadness about them. In the middle of that blazing Indian summer afternoon, he took my hand and helped me to the car. He is a pediatrician and good in such matters. George and I come from the same place, a suburb that borders on farmland on the northern shores of Lake Michigan. One night when we were still really children, he borrowed his father's car and drove me down to the lake. We took off our shoes and socks and jumped the picket fence, which wasn't very tall. We walked, holding hands, along the beach, and the lake lapped at our feet. This was before the fish started dying and the water was still clean, though the thaw had just come and it was ice cold.

We sat on a dune and started burying ourselves in the sand. I never saw such a black night. There wasn't a star, no moon. I could hear the lake and knew it was there, but what I saw ahead of me seemed empty, and the waves as they broke seemed to come from nowhere. George tried to kiss me but I got up and ran. Racing back to the car, I tripped over two pairs of feet. I mumbled an apology, but the boy and girl who lay in the sand scrambled away like frightened crabs. George tackled me and I said I wanted to go to the car.

In the car I put my feet in his lap. We were slumped down with the radio blaring and George started counting my toes.

That's what he was doing when the police arrived, but they never believed us. We knew it was the police because they broke the unspoken code. The code is, when you drive down to the lake at night, you cut your lights if other cars are parked, but they kept their brights coming all the way. They shone searchlights in our faces and made George stand spread-eagled against the car while they searched him, for what I'll never know. "No-good kids," one of them said. "I know troublemakers when I see them."

It was fate, George said, that made him remember my grandmother's unreal last name, with its *j*'s and *z*'s, like some winning Scrabble word. When I said I wouldn't go out for dinner with him the next night, he said we could order in. For the time I was home, I persuaded my family to let me stay in my grandmother's apartment, where she'd lived alone for the forty-odd years of her widowhood. I knew I was the one to put her things in order, because I'd traveled with her to Florida and was always with her when she visited the animals. I was also the last one to see her alive. I was bound to her, perhaps more than any other member of the clan, whose extended numbers reached into the hundreds. My grandmother was keeper of the family archive; she had the classificatory abilities of a Linnaeus and knew where everyone was and with whom. She came to America with a dozen brothers and sisters. There had been four sets of twins, and some of the twins never married but lived until they died with their twin. My grandmother's twin died of pneumonia when she was three weeks old. She was the only child who died young on that side of the family, and I am named for her. I've always felt myself bound to my grandmother as twins are bound.

The next night George watched patiently as I started sorting my grandmother's things. He'd come straight from the office and arrived in a bad mood. I told him to relax and he took off his jacket, tie, and cuff links. He hung up his jacket and tie and left the cuff links on the dresser. He took off his shoes and flopped on the bed, listening to the news. I laid out the boas, an old lace-up corset, high-button shoes. I started putting on her things. The lace-up corset, which George helped me tighten over my clothes, felt like a straitjacket. A call came in for Dr. Ringer. George spoke in a muffled voice, and I could tell from his eyes that he was making a terrible diagnosis. Then my parents called. "You shouldn't stay there alone," my mother said. I told her I wasn't alone. "It's not right. There are people who want to see you." She held the receiver in the air so that I could hear the rumblings of relatives in the background. My father snatched the phone from her hands. "What are you doing there by yourself?" I told him I had company. "What kind of company?" he grumbled. It was my mother's mother who had died, but my father was as irritable as he was when anything threatened to touch him personally. I couldn't tell him I was with George; he still held it against George that he'd gotten me booked on a vagrancy charge fifteen years ago and that because of him I held a police record. I evoked instead old girlfriends, wives living now in the suburbs, who'd left husbands and children to share my grief.

After talking to my father, I accidentally packed George's cuff links away with my grandmother's jewelry. We spent part of the evening searching for them, because I had no recollection of putting them away. They were a gift from a woman he'd just stopped living with and he said they had sentimental value. They were solid gold cuff links with an Indian chief in full headdress carved on them, a once great warrior perhaps, the kind from old nickels or the fronts of trading posts. I could tell by how badly he wanted to find them that the woman was still somehow important to him, but I didn't ask about her. I just helped him look.

After we found them in the box I'd packed them in, he relaxed. He phoned Shanghai and ordered Cantonese food. He liked sweet and sour shrimp crisp with a special sauce, and he pressed my ear to the phone so that I could hear the man say "Yesa, Doca Linga." When the shrimp arrived, I decided we couldn't eat it on my grandmother's plates — kosher for seventy-five years. George said I was being sentimental about something I didn't believe in, but I told him I didn't think he was being sentimental about his cuff links. He knew he didn't have a leg to stand on, so he went out for paper plates and plastic forks. While he was gone, I missed him. I hadn't missed a man for a long time, and it seemed as if we'd finally been brought together so many years after two policemen, with nothing better to do, had wrenched us apart.

After dinner we turned on my grandmother's television set and stretched out on the four-poster. Little wood nymphs, hand carved, stood guard on top of each poster. My mother said it was a pagan bed and the antithesis of my grandmother. My only girl cousin and I used to build forts out of pillows and blankets to keep the Indians away. It was a big bed, and lying on it I always felt I had to shout to be heard. George knew I didn't want to be alone, so he agreed to spend the night. He was very tired and slept in his clothes on top of the covers. I slept with my head on his arm, and periodically he clasped me to him like a child with a rag doll. He ran his fingers through my hair as if he were looking for something. We'd never been lovers, and I'm fairly certain it hadn't crossed our minds when we were younger. George played baseball for Ohio during college, and two or three times a year during the season he came to play in Boston and he stayed with me. One afternoon when the magnolias were blooming, we walked toward Harvard Square, wandering to the address of another high school friend who that same afternoon was killing himself and his girlfriend on Cape Cod. There was also a total eclipse of the sun that day, and George often said it was the eclipse that made our friend go mad. We carried salami sandwiches and a smoky glass down to the banks of the Charles and, with every other student from the Cambridge side of the river who'd never seen a complete solar eclipse, we peered at the flaming corona as the moon crossed in front of and, for a brief instant, blotted out the sun.

My cousin Sammy rang the doorbell the next morning and accused me of gold digging. What was there to dig for here? He said he was going to put an injunction on me so that I couldn't touch any of the stuff. "Sammy," I said, "I'm just packing. The lawyer will decide."

"You'd better get yourself a lawyer, you little thief."

Sammy and I hadn't been on great terms since my mother stopped talking to her brother, Sammy's father. I phoned Bill Swallow, my grandmother's attorney, and told him I was putting things in order because my mother had told me to. I felt strange, citing parental permission. My grandmother left nothing but her belongings, but Mr. Swallow was very sympathetic and said he'd give me legal permission to be there. The next morning Sammy appeared with two suitcases. "Are you going on a trip?" I asked. He barged in and started packing away towels, porcelain, whatever caught his eye. He'd always been a troublemaker and had never held a steady job. Bill Swallow agreed to meet me for lunch to put an injunction on him.

He expected a much younger woman, one who might need parental permission, and I a much older man. In fact, I was slightly older than he, but he was very serious for his years. He wore a man's hat and rubbers because it had recently rained. When he handed the hatcheck girl his rubbers, she held them between two fingers as if she had a dead rat by the tail. His hair was perfectly trimmed, exactly an inch too short all the way around. He seemed to speak Latin when he talked. "I will gladly detain your grandmother's possessions in probate," he said after a martini, his hand slipping over mine. I was certain he'd fallen in love with me at first sight. I pulled my hand away. "I only meant to console," he said, and I agreed to have dinner with him some time during the week.

George came over that evening. "I saw you having lunch with some guy over at Cricket's. He looked like an attorney."

"My grandmother's," I said. "You should've said hello."

"Sure," George replied, "and I'm the family doctor."

We went to the North Star Inn, an old mob hangout, and George whispered to me the names of everyone in the place with Mafia ties, which seemed to be the majority of the clientele — real leg breakers. They're a family, too, I thought. When I started to cry, George stretched his hands across the table and I clutched them the way I've seen actors do in movies when someone's taking the bullet from their thigh. I've always admired doctors, as if they, like psychics, see a part of ourselves we can never see — though George has told me that all they see are torn sinews and clogged vessels. My grandmother had little faith in doctors. I was home for a wedding when she called and said she wanted to go to the hospital. We didn't even know she was sick. The admitting intern asked questions, which he said were routine: "Are your parents living? When was the date of your last period?" Around 1929, she said, and my mother and I couldn't stop laughing.

On Saturday I persuaded George to drive north. I wanted to follow the Hiawatha Trail as it wound around the lake and see the leaves before they fell. I wanted to pass houses where girlfriends had hit a boundless and unexplained puberty and where boys first knew their powers in darkened rooms when we were all supposed to be baby-sitting for younger siblings. I wanted to see the old house again, now with a flagpole stuck in the lawn, and then have a mushroom and sausage pizza at Scornavacco's. George said I was nuts, but he drove. He drove past the Bahai Temple — which, one beer-drinking Friday night in a convertible in 1963, just after his mother died, he'd dubbed God's orange-juice squeezer because of its scalloped domes, and we laughed about vitamin C pouring down from heaven. When we reached Glencoe, I saw sweat on the back of his neck. "Are you sick?" I asked. He shook his head, but the fine features of his face seemed to grow smaller, as if they would disappear into his head. His hands gripped the wheel. His neck was glossy, as if he were being thawed. He pulled over. "Look" — he patted my cheek — "I don't want to go back there." He told me that now, some fifteen years later, he couldn't go home. "Sometimes if I have to go there, I feel like the house could actually keep me from leaving. My father still lives there alone." His father slept in the same bed where his wife had died.

We swung off County Line Road and headed back to the city on Edens, and George's mood shifted as the distance between our town and us increased. He talked about Elena, the one who'd given him the cuff links. "She was crazy about details. A spot on my tie became a character flaw." She pursued him with a missionary's zeal. Her calls were relentless; he hadn't slept in weeks. Sometimes he glanced over his shoulder, only to find that the wind was following at his back. They'd lived together for over a year, but she didn't quite fit the image. He told me, matter-of-factly, that I didn't either. "So far no one has." He kept tucked away in the corners of his mind — the way old athletes keep scrapbooks of all they've been and, late at night when no one is around, flip through them — an image of the woman he would eventually love. He couldn't describe her, but he knew he'd know her when he saw her, and he knew he'd see her. His mother used to tell him that dreams spilled over into reality; this was before he'd watched her dreams crumble. The doorman held the door open for me, and George, refusing a nightcap, kissed me on the crown of my head.

I thought I saw my grandmother as I let myself in. She was coming down the corridor in her blue robe to meet me, forgetting I had my own key. Her hand guided her along the dark hallway for a moment and then she was gone. I turned on the television to bring the real world back into the living room. The news forecast snow for the end of the week. When I was a child, I used to be afraid of snowstorms, because I thought the snow could, if it wanted to, fall all at once instead of fluttering down — that it could hit with a thud.

As the late show began, I heard shouting. It wasn't coming from the television. I walked through the apartment, lighting every light to see if the noise came from within the apartment. I put on my nightgown and returned to the living room, but the shouting started again. A woman shrieked. A man hollered. I went to the door and peeked from the peephole but saw nothing. The woman was shouting again. I traced the sound to the studio next door, and feeling a need to eavesdrop on other people's problems, I leaned out, my foot bracing the door. The man yelled; the woman yelled back. There was a crashing sound. I leaned out farther, hoping to catch the details. Did she not fit his image? Or he hers? Was he frightened? Or was she? Or was it something more mundane — a petty jealousy, a wrong word spoken over dinner? And was I now, somehow, like my grandmother, an observer of other people's lives? I leaned farther, trying to decide if I was getting old, and the door slipped from my foot, slamming shut behind me. I stood in the middle of the hallway, barefoot and bewildered in a semitransparent gown. I couldn't take the elevator to the lobby. How would the doorman view my nakedness? Would he tell my mother? He probably had a daughter my age.

I knocked on the door of the arguing couple during a lull in the fight. A complete silence fell over their apartment. Then I heard muffled whispers. "Now you did it," the woman said. "Somebody called the cops."

"Excuse me." I pressed my lips to the door. "I'm your neighbor and I'm locked out." The door opened suspiciously. "Could I use your phone?" The first thing I saw was the overflowing ashtray, then the heap of beer cans against the balcony doors, the rumpled sheets of the sofa-bed. A bleary-eyed, balding man with forehead creases poked his head at me. My hands went instinctively to cover my breasts. He tugged at his GIMME SHELTER T-shirt. He wore boxer shorts. Slumped in the armchair like a tattered stuffed animal was my grandmother's frosty-haired neighbor, not much older than myself, I suspected, but looking the worse for wear. "I'm sorry," I mumbled. "I heard voices and thought something was wrong." They exchanged doubting glances.

"I can't believe you locked yourself out," George said, wrapping me in an overcoat. I couldn't either. "It's not at all like you." I agreed. I was grateful he'd answered the phone, knowing he usually just stared at it if there was a late-night call, unless his service beeped him. He said he knew it was me. The man in his boxer shorts tried to elbow the door down. George worked at it with some tools he'd brought. "You'd better come home with me," he said. I could get a passkey from the doorman in the morning. The fighting couple disappeared back into their studio. "You did this on purpose," George said, carrying me to the car discreetly out the back door. In his car, I tucked my legs up to my chin. Maybe I did do it on purpose. Maybe I wanted to fight to the bitter end with someone in his boxer shorts. George's features, which had always seemed to me so dark and fine, again grew smaller and smaller. His pupils contracted as if they would disappear into his head, as if in the face of a blinding light. All women had become potential Elenas to him, making crazy late-night calls. As we zipped along the drive, I wondered if I was confusing memory with feeling. Just because you know a person, a place, for a long time doesn't mean you know him well. Maybe because it was all so familiar — this lake, this cold, corrupt city, the man driving beside me — maybe because I was barefoot in November in a man's coat like a bag lady, I thought that I wanted George as much as I'd ever wanted anything.

He had a bachelor pad with wall-to-wall carpeting and no furniture. The plants sat baking on the radiator like incubating infants, and I made him put them all in the shower. I curled up in George's bed, and when he lay down, I rested my head again on his shoulder. I was about to press against his thigh when the phone started to ring. It rang four times and stopped. George stared at the phone as if it were a three-headed monster. It started to ring again, and after I counted fifteen rings, I got up to answer it. At twenty-one rings I crossed the wall-to-wall carpeting, and when George didn't tell me not to, I picked up the phone.

"Hello, hello." A woman's voice was faint at the other end.

"Can I help you?" I said after a pause. Suddenly I was consumed with empathy for the disembodied voice of a woman I'd never met who made late-night calls, I myself having just done the same. "It's all right," I whispered. "You can talk to me."

"I don't want to talk to you," she said.

What was this other woman like? I pictured a chain-smoker with long, yellow hair that she spun nervously around her index finger; B.A. Western Illinois, in public relations. George sat stone-faced on the bed. The truth was, and I knew it, that Elena was like any other person. She paid bills and drank brandy. She went to the Caribbean when she could scrape together the money. She had brothers and sisters and nail polish on her nails. There wasn't a visible desperate bone in her body when she went to the supermarket. Searching for comforting words, I said, "Listen, it's not what you think."

"I know he's there!" she shouted at me. "Tell him I'm going to kill myself."

I thrust my hand over the receiver. "She's going to kill herself."

George flicked his hand at me. "So what else is new?"

Once I'd worked on a hot line. Keep them talking, I'd been told. "You don't have to worry," I said to her. "He's just afraid, like everyone else. He doesn't know what he wants." She yelled something at me and hung up.

"She's into persecution," George said. At first he too was alarmed; now it'd become a habit. "She didn't want me when I wanted her. Now she's going crazy." The power we have over others' lives, I thought. "I'm not a bottomless pit," George said.

The next afternoon he had time to kill, so we went touring the city. We walked east on Madison, taking in the Loop's main scent, that of caramel corn, and the perpetual line of poor people waiting to bring it home. The weather was starting to turn. Chicagoans have a stoical attitude toward winter. They tighten their lips and go about their business. The city was born of snow; its beaches and marshes are Ice Age, late Pleistocene. We found this out at the Field Museum, where George took me to see the bones of dinosaurs that had wandered Lake Michigan when it was a mere bowl holding a glacier in its cup. We stood beneath a dinothere, a sad elephant with useless, inverted tusks that never served to protect him. Lines of schoolchildren filed by, their voices echoing through the great hall. George's hand went instinctively to his neck; he was having one of his phantom pains. He'd had them ever since I met him, when we were just finishing grammar school. He suffered in many of the same places where his mother had suffered. He put an arm around me. When he was the same age as those schoolchildren, he told me, his mother used to bring him here and she'd stand crying under the bones. But the trip to the museum was only an excuse. She made him go with her whenever she went to the doctor. In this way, George admitted, she bound him to her illness — and to everyone else's.

"I'm tired of looking after other people's babies," he confessed as we walked out of the museum. He'd made a lot of money the previous year in stock options and speculations. "I'm going to buy land in Mexico," he declared as we drove along the drive.

Thinking he meant to settle down, I said, "To build a house?"

"No," he said. "To start drilling." It was petroleum that preoccupied him. He was ready to invest in petropesos. He wanted to dip his fingers into pure, black, combustible slime. He wanted to wallow in it like a pig in the muck. I told him he was crazy. "Medicine isn't the noble profession it's cut out to be," he said as we pulled into the parking garage. "Every day I see terrible things." The garage attendant stuck a number on our windshield. George clasped my hand. "Lawyers and doctors, we're overestimated and overpaid. Lawyers don't save the world." On the contrary, he said, civilization's been tied up in the courts for years. "But we could perform a real service." He held my hand tighter. We'd buy a clump of uninhabitable jungle in Chiapas, where roads hadn't yet reached; he had a divining rod for a brain.

I wasn't convinced as I followed him into the old Downtown Branch of the Chicago Public Library. George dashed off toward the card catalogue to find books to show me what energy could do. I wandered into the main reading room. This particular room always had a special place in my heart that I never shared with anyone. My father would bring me down with him on the train, and I used to study under the stained-glass windows in this expansive room during my Christmas breaks. I entered high school when I was eleven. A well-dressed man with tortoiseshell glasses and aging navy suits, who read thick accounting books with tiny print, used to sit beside me and expose himself. It happened perhaps a half-dozen times that year. He always came at lunchtime and sat beside me. He'd lean over and ask, "What are you reading?" Books were no use to me in solving the problem of this man. I knew something was wrong, but I wasn't sure why. I was impressed by his terribly lonely eyes, not unlike those of the great ape Bushman. I had never seen a man aroused before, and it perplexed me; I thought he was deformed by disease and perhaps unzipped his fly to relieve some hideous pressure I could only faintly understand. In the end it was the regularity of his appearance that frightened me, and when at last I went to the guard, the CPA — for that's what I now assume he was — snatched up his books and dashed, like a hunted thing, from the library. I knew exactly where I used to sit — the far left-hand seat in the tenth row of tables beside the social studies section. I found that seat and sat down, waiting for George.

I had been preparing a research report that Christmas on the life of a soybean, an interesting life with endless possibilities. The soybean is one of our most versatile plants.

The purple flowers, the brown, hairy pods. Why can't women be exhibitionists, I wondered? Why aren't there lady flashers? A group of widows from Indiana, obviously with some church-organized tour, flaccid matrons in polyesters with patent-leather shoes, passed by, and I focused on one. She wore a green and pink striped shirtwaist and dark pumps, and I tried to picture her hiking up her skirts, sending some young man shrieking across a sand dune or out of a men's room.

The seat to my right where the pervert always sat was pulled back, and George sat down, shoving books on oil wells in front of me. He showed me a picture. Oil spewing from the sky, riggers catching it like moonbeams in their hands. "It's energy that keeps America running," he said. At that moment I wanted to press him to me, to rid him of fantastic schemes, terrible fears, the memory of illness. Instead, I let my hand rest across his arm and he held my fingers in a comfortable intimacy. "Solar power's more like it," I told him, zapping rays from our own private star. Oil's depressing: all that animal juice, our crushed remains.

My grandmother never had much use for men, and after she was widowed, though she had many offers, she stayed single. She had wanted to be a dancer, but first her father, then her husband, refused. She was an ethereal woman who seemed to embody the qualities of a soap bubble, frail and transparent, leaving the impression that the wind, not her heart, would carry her away. We worried when she walked out into a windy Chicago day, half blind, taking the bus to Marshall Field's when they had a pistachio ice cream sale. Sometimes, she confessed, she'd go out just so that young men would help her cross the street, because, though she didn't marry, she liked to flirt. Still, I wasn't prepared to find a packet of love letters, neatly tied with a pink ribbon, in a bottom drawer. When she was in her eighties, she had told me, "Men aren't so great, you know." I didn't know. All the letters in the package were from the same man, written in the same hand. "Dearest," I read, "it has been two weeks since we spoke, longer since I've seen you." I scanned the letter for a signature but found none. I fantasized a married man. I skimmed. "Though I realize the limitations of my station and affection for you, though I see how awkward my approach must seem, I do not feel inside me this awkwardness. What I feel, I believe, is genuine." I read the remainder of the letters — all variations on the same theme, the anonymous man's longing, her evasiveness. The voice reminded me of Bill Swallow, so I wasn't surprised when the phone rang as I read and it was he, reminding me we had plans for that evening. I'd been lost among another's possessions for days, it seemed, and had forgotten my grandmother's attorney. I made an excuse that I had much to tend to in the apartment, and we agreed he'd come over and we'd order in.

Bill left his rubbers in the hallway. "Terrible rain," he said, handing me his hat. I phoned Shanghai and ordered sweet and sour shrimp. When I gave the man the address, he said, "Shall I do it da way Doca Linga like it?"

"Yes," I said, "do it the way he likes it." In the middle of dinner, Bill gripped my hand and said I was the woman of his dreams. Lawyers have a knack for getting to the point. To think I could play a lead role in the nights of someone I scarcely knew was startling, and he saw in my eyes that he'd put me off. "I didn't mean to frighten you," he said. "It's just that I've been looking for someone like you for a long time and I know you're what I want."

"You're hardly thirty," I told him. Of course he knew nothing about me, beyond the surface, but maybe that was all I knew of George. Bill blushed and lit a Pall Mall. "And you don't know me."

"I know enough," he said flatly. Maybe he did know enough. But he didn't fit my image; he wanted a wife who'd live in the suburbs and shop at Sunset. George fitted my image, if only for continuity's sake, as if he held my childhood in those pediatric hands. Even the man from Shanghai linked us together. "Won't you at least consider staying a little longer?" Bill said. "Then I could get to know you more." I said I'd consider it if my paper gave me more time off.

That night, as I slept, a huge crash woke me. I thought we'd been bombed — but who'd bomb Chicago, especially this block? What secrets needed to be destroyed here? Another crash came, and I knew it was a thief, boring his way into the once protected walls. I crawled into a ball under the covers, hoping whoever it was would mistake me for an unmade bed. Another crash came, from the bathroom it seemed, followed by a settling sound. I waited for what felt like hours. Every shadow was a masked man, every light from the street a burglar's flashlight. I was afraid that, if I opened my eyes, a foglike image would appear in the mirror and I'd have to comply with its most ludicrous wishes. Finally I switched on the light. Dust rose from beneath the bathroom door. When I opened the door, I saw, lying in a heap on the floor, the bathroom ceiling.

The plumber explained that for years a slow leak in the hot-water pipe above the tub had seeped water, like reaching fingers into the weakening plaster, separating it from the pipes until finally it caved in. George came over in the evening. "What a mess," he said, peering in. He took off his tie, jacket, and cuff links. He watched television while I packed, this time my things — for I suspected, in a superstitious moment, that the bathroom ceiling was intended as a warning for me to get away. Maybe if I was gone, he'd come looking for me. I curled up in George's arms and slept. I had a vague recollection of him kissing me at dawn and of him whispering he'd miss me. When I woke, he'd left for the hospital. While dressing, I found his cuff links on the dresser, where he'd forgotten them. I wrapped them in tinfoil, stuffed them in a brown paper bag with a note that read, "I'll always remember my head on your arm. Thank you for staying here." I phoned him. "They'll be with the doorman," I said.

"Is there a note?" He didn't seem to care about the cuff links. I said of course there was a note. "Then I'll get them right after work." He paused. "I really will miss you." I knew he would. I knew after work he'd pick up the package from the doorman, he'd read the note, and the chain of events would continue after I'd gone, and he'd think of me, the way I'd think of him. I stapled the paper bag shut and put George's name on it; the doorman thought I was leaving him a child's lunch.

Once you grow accustomed to them, distances don't seem so great. I've made this trip a hundred times. The plane lifts me into the air and we climb above the layer of cumulonimbus clouds, the artist's conception of heaven. I think of souls rising. Every time I go back east, I relive my life in the plane, like the embryo repeating the history of its race in the womb. I leave crying. Somewhere over Ohio, my adolescence begins. By the time we're circling La-Guardia, I'm on the brink of a somewhat somber adulthood. The year before, I'd left my grandmother in front of her hotel, waving at me. She wore a dark blue dress with white flowers, and blended into the water and sky behind her. There were mostly students on my midnight flight, and the pilot greeted us over the loudspeaker: "Good evening, ladies and gentlemen. This is your pilot, Captain Crasher, welcoming you aboard." Nervous laughter tittered through the cabin as we ordered more drinks. Either a sick joke or the words of a madman. I saw no omens.

I had been back for more than a week when my mother phoned. We had a brief conversation — the usual kind, in which she asks questions and I answer yes or no. She always wants to know everything, as if details could provide intimacy. If I try to turn the conversation around and ask her questions, she always says, "Oh, nothing's new. Dullsville around here." I try to explain, when she resumes her questioning, that I've grown up and I'll tell her what I want her to know. She quickly switches topics. "I went to close up the apartment today." She sighed. "You can't imagine how much I wanted you with me." The movers came and all the furniture went to a resale warehouse. "I saved you the eggbeater and some pots." Bill Swallow had gotten everything smoothly through probate. "He asked about you," she said. "I think he likes you. I gave him your address." She also gave Sammy whatever he wanted, to avoid a fight.

One of the movers slammed the old bed into a wall, and one of the rare, hand-carved posters snapped in half. She said she'd cried her heart out. And as she was leaving, the doorman handed her a package, the one I'd left for the man who was supposed to pick it up. "I opened it," she said, "to see what was inside." She had no business opening it, and we both knew that. It was a sealed package between adults, one of whom had broken his part of the bargain. I also knew she'd read the note, which she didn't mention, thanking George for letting me sleep in his arms, and that she'd misunderstood its meaning.

"What'll I do with the cuff links?" she asked. She sounded perplexed and exasperated. When I told her to throw them out, she protested in a high-pitched voice, "But they're gold."

"Look, I'll tell George to pick them up. All right?"

"Good, that's good." She was excessively relieved; I might as well have said I saw Grandma last night and she

looked just fine to me. What my mother needed was continuity, the sense that things would go on as they'd always
been. But my grandmother was dead and George had not
come for his cuff links and some things would just not be
what they'd been. Or could have been. I sank into obsti-
nate silence. "Tell him to come by in the evening, all right?"
she went on. "After dinner. We can have a little chat."

I didn't say anything. My mother paused, breathing
deeply, as if this were some obscene call she'd just made,
and I listened to her breathe across the seemingly endless
stretch of midwestern plain.

Burning Issues

T HIS IS WHAT I always come back to, Evelyn thinks, as she tries to wake the children. I always come back to that night when Mars came down and kissed the earth the way Walt said and we couldn't wake them up then, either. The children can sleep through anything. They always have.

The toast pops up but it's still pale, so she shoves it down the way she'd like to shove other things down. It goes in easily and she watches it, disappearing into the toaster, the light of the toaster warming her hand. She'll have to go back upstairs and wake them, but she knows it's useless. In the morning when they were going to school, she used to dread waking them. She'd bang on pots or drop cold water on their heads. She's never slept the way they do.

She's always waked at the slightest sound, a little rustling beside her, a truck passing. She hadn't even been able to wake them the night when the collies were born and she and Walt wanted them to come and see the dog lick the sacs off and bite off the cord or the night when the ex-con tried to break in and the police had come. Or when Mars had come down so close to the earth.

The toast stings her fingers as she plucks it from the toaster. It's charred this time, and she thinks she should throw it out. Instead, she scrapes the burned part off with a knife. It's not her fault, she tells herself as she butters the bread. She likes to watch the butter as it softens and spreads, opening into rivulets on the toast. She'd been that way in Walt's hands, like butter on warm bread. She likes to watch it melt the way she liked to watch the ice melt when the first thaw came. She'd always wanted him to take her to a warm climate. She had read somewhere that some people are like alligators and their blood adjusted to the temperature of the air, but she knew she wasn't one of them. The winter chills always entered her bones, and she could never get warm enough in the north. She'd have lived at the equator if Walt had wanted to move there.

She calls once more, and as she begins to walk to the stairs, she hears rumbling above. This time they call back, their voices hardly the voices of children anymore. They'd looked huge last night when she tucked them into their enormous baby beds.

It was late, and they had fallen right to sleep. Evelyn tried to read but couldn't, and she'd gone back into Laura's room to see if she was still awake. But Laura had fallen sound asleep the minute her head hit the pillow. Laura had always been that way. She didn't want to go back to it, but she couldn't help it. She went back again to the night when Mars had almost come down and touched the earth. When the red planet was big in the sky as a football. She and Walt had shaken each one of them in their beds and, finally giving up, had just gone into the backyard themselves and watched Mars like a big fireball overhead.

She burns the eggs. She's forgotten about them and they sit in the old iron pan, frothy and smoky. She turns them, and dark crusts of egg appear. She debates throwing out the eggs, but it's not her fault. It's theirs for not waking up. And she has to blame that picture of Walt, sitting there on the windowsill in the sunlight. The light coming through his eyes, his mouth, coming right out of him, at that hour of the morning. Just at breakfast time. In the corners of the Lucite frame, little rainbows appear.

Sometimes she asks the picture what she should do. Sell the house? Move south? The light animates his face, as if he's smiling at her. She noticed it the other morning and it made her shudder. As if he's somehow trapped inside in that Lucite frame and he can't get to her, like that TV show she saw once when someone was trapped inside the pistons of his own automobile.

He'd looked that way, the light in his eyes, the night when Mars came closest to the earth. It was the closest the planet had been in four hundred years, and it wouldn't come that close again for another four hundred. It was once in a lifetime, so they'd tried to wake the children, but they couldn't. So they'd taken a blanket and they'd lain down on it and watched as the planet pulsated, blue and red, and it seemed to vibrate above them.

It seemed so close and fiery, they'd almost expected it to say something to them, but it just hung overhead like a blessing. And after watching a while, Walt had curled up beside her and whispered into her ear. He'd said, "I want you." And that night was burned into memory. It wasn't like the other thousands of nights. That one stood out as if he'd reached farther into her than anyone ever could, so that she knew this was where she belonged. The ground had felt dewy and cold, even with the blanket under them. And his hot breath on her neck had wedded her to him, like a brand on a cow.

Upstairs she hears the children, rumbling in the bathroom, washing their faces, brushing their teeth. Big children, huge children now. The children so huge, she can't imagine how they ever came out of her. It seems impossible, but somehow they did. Burst out of her one day when she thought she'd explode. And one, Sam, had come so fast, he had spilled out into Walt's hands on the way to the hospital. Walt had grabbed the baby in his hands, wrapped him in his own shirt, and said the baby was a little hot potato. That was what Walt had said. He'd called the baby a hot potato as he slipped into his hands.

They come downstairs in their pajamas, all grown now, like the zucchini seeds she'd planted a few years before when monster zucchini grew. They've flown in from cities east and west, and she watches as they clomp downstairs. They come close and touch her, cheeks moist with sleep, then move away.

"Your breakfast is getting cold," she tells them. They sit down obediently and swallow their grief. They eat cold toast, burned eggs, seared bacon. She probably should throw it all out, she thinks, and begin again.

About the Author

Mary Morris is the author of a collection of short stories, *Vanishing Animals and Other Stories* (Godine, 1979), which was awarded the Rome Fellowship in Literature by the American Academy and Institute of Arts and Letters, and a novel, *Crossroads* (Houghton Mifflin, 1983). She teaches at Princeton University and lives in New York City.